THE UNICORNS'
FORTUNE

© 2019
Herstellung und Verlag: BoD – Books on Demand, Norderstedt.

ISBN: 9783746078151

This book is a human-horse novel.
It is a story about the bond of women and their horses,
and the bliss that horses bring to one's life.
The story entails sagas of the unicorn that evidently
show the fascination of people all over the world about
horses, and their life-power that made them a symbol of
life and a popular emblem.
It is a book for horse-lovers of all ages, children, young
people, old people and everyone in between.
It touches themes like finding one's path and one's
calling, one's roots and making peace with one's history
in order to start following one's dreams.

Dedicated

To my grandmother, my mother and our magic horse.

CONTENTS

THE MISSION

*O*n Mary Rose's eighteenth birthday, the First of January 2001, her grandmother asked her to fulfill her last wish. Mary Rose had always had the feeling that her grandmother was training and teaching her. She had taught her all of life's lessons. But Mary Rose had always had a feeling that there was something else, something she had never told her, something kept secret.

Outside the window of the cottage, a snow storm was howling. In front of the window snow blew across the Scottish headland. Inside the cottage it was nice and warm. A fire was crackling. It smelled of freshly brewed tea and home-made bread that was still in the oven.

Her grandmother called her name.

Mary Rose sensed that there was something important to come when she entered the living room. Her grandmother sat in her old wooden rocking chair at the fireplace. Even though she was old, she still was beautiful, Mary Rose thought. Her hair was white with a silver and golden sheen, just like the fur of her white horses. In the light of the flickering fire, her eyes sparkled. Mary Rose sat down in the chair next to her at the fireplace in the living room and looked at grandmother Annemarie expectantly.

"Mary Rose, my dear, I have to ask you for a favour."

"Anything, Granny, I will do anything for you."

"Oh sweet Mary Rose, you are special. You are the kind of person the world needs more of."

"So are you, granny Annemarie."

Grandmother Annemarie smiled.

A silence followed. Annemarie looked at her granddaughter for a while. Her eyes were somehow tired, but they still had this gentle, generous and grateful expression to them, that was so characteristic of Annemarie. They sparkled in the flickering light of the crackling fire. Her face looked tired as her glance wandered off and she looked out of the window into the snow storm that swept across the headland. When she turned back to Mary Rose, she had a gentle smile on her face.

Mary Rose looked at her grandmother curiously, she had no idea what was to come. What was it that her grandmother had to ask her?

Her Grandmother spoke solemnly:

"My dearest granddaughter, I ask you to fulfill my last wish." She paused for a moment.

Mary Rose was shocked. Whilst she struggled to grasp the meaning of these words, she felt numb, her knees felt weak and she sank to the ground in front of her grandmother. Then a wave of emotion overcame her and she felt her heart become heavy and her eyes filled with tears. She kneeled right in front of her with eyes wide open. She stared at her grandmother but she was too shocked to say a word.

Annemarie gently stroke over her hair and smiled at her granddaughter. Then she continued:

"Even though there is nothing harder for me than to let you go, I have to send you away. I have to send you on a mission."

Mary Rose was surprised. 'A mission?' She still could not guess what her grandmother's last wish could be, and was filled with curiosity.

Grandmother Annemarie took her hands and held them, then she spoke to her intensely.

"Return the fortune of the unicorn to the woman who gave it to me in my hour of need. Return what we received and repay my debt. Return the gift and bring these blessings back to my saviour. Go and tell her the story I told you a hundred times. Go and tell the world the story of the unicorns' fortune."

'That was it!' Mary Rose thought by herself. 'That is, what granny Annemarie had on her mind all those years! I knew there was something that was bothering her for a lifetime. So that's what it is. She wants me to bring back the fortune of the unicorn to the woman who gave it to her.'

Mary Rose was shocked and touched at the same time. It took her by surprise. She had never guessed it, even though, now that grandmother Annemarie told her it seemed obvious. Mary Rose understood, she knew why.

A storm of thoughts and feelings swept through her. Mary Rose was scared and sad as she realised that she suppressed the thought that her grandmother will not live eternally. She felt great appreciation and understanding for her wish. And she felt proud and nervous at the same time that she was chosen to fulfil her grandmother's last wish.

"Darling, you know, it is difficult for me to put such a burden and such a journey on you but I just cannot rest in peace without thanking that woman. I want her to know what she has done for me. You are the only one who truly understands that. You must do it."

Mary Rose felt a bit dizzy. Many thoughts swirled through her head just like the snowflakes outside the window. She felt a storm of emotions coming up inside her - fear and sadness over the thought that her beloved grandmother would die one day, she was deeply moved over her grandmother's wish to return the precious gift she once had received, and she was a bit worried and scared thinking that she would be responsible to make sure the gift was returned. She felt nervous, but she wanted to be brave. She took a deep breath and nodded. Then she said with a strong voice:

"It is a great honour for me to bring the fortune of the unicorn back to the woman who gave it to you. I know how brave she was, how generous, and I know, that you owe her your life. I fully understand. The fortune shall be given back."

Mary Rose paused for a moment. Then she continued:

"I think I am destined for this mission. I have been waiting years for you to tell me what the secret was that you were keeping from me. Now I know, it is this wish to take up this journey once more and return what needs to be returned. I will do my best to complete it."

Grandmother Annemarie gave her granddaughter a gentle smile. She was proud of her. Mary Rose was still kneeling on the ground in front of her grandmother's rocking chair. Annemarie was still holding Mary Rose's hands. Then she spoke to her with a whispering voice.

"You were kissed by the unicorn when you were a little child."

Mary Rose smiled. Then she replied:

"I've been blessed with a unicorn whispering grandmother and her magic unicorns."

That made grandmother Annemarie smile. She whispered:

"Let me kiss your forehead my darling!"

Mary Rose bowed in front of her grandmother. It felt like a ceremony. In that ceremony, grandmother Annemarie was the queen, and she knighted her granddaughter with the blessings of love. She kissed her forehead and then she announced:

"Mary Rose, you are a grown woman now, you have learned everything I know, and more. At your young age, you are already a greater unicorn whisperer than I have ever been. You are smart, brave and strong. You are a knight of the unicorn now."

Mary Rose regained her composure. She stood up. She truly felt like she had been knighted. She felt honoured that her grandmother had chosen her to complete this mission.

Grandmother Annemarie handed her three items with her shaking hand: a letter for the woman, a book consisting of a few hand-sewn, worn out pages that made up the diary which she had written during her journey to Scotland; and a package that Mary Rose should open only upon her return to Scotland.

Mary Rose took the items carefully. But then she could not hold back her feelings any longer and she burst out:

"Grandma, I am honoured to go on this mission. I am grateful that you chose me. I am confident I shall be successful. But what worries me is that you are asking me to fulfill your 'last' wish. I hope that doesn't mean that you are planning to leave soon. How can I live without you?"

"Darling Mary Rose! Do not worry about me. I promise to stay with you for as long as I can. But when my time comes, I will have to go. And you will have to let me go. You will know that I will be relieved after you have fulfilled my last wish."

She paused for a moment and looked at the worried face of her granddaughter. She smiled gently, then she continued:

"I will always be with you. I will be in every horse that you see. And most of all, I am in you. Mary Rose, you are my pride and I know I will live on in your heart. I cannot even express how much I love you and how grateful I am for every second I am with you. And I will live on in your heart and in the horses' hearts."

Mary Rose had tears in her eyes. She nodded. She tried to fight the tears and be brave. She gave her grand-mother a hug.

Her grandmother smiled at her lovingly. Then she sighed and leaned back in the rocking chair. She looked tired.

Mary Rose tried to swallow down the tears, but she just couldn't. She turned around slowly and walked upstairs where she fell onto her bed. She couldn't imagine a life without her grandmother. She cried, but knew she had to be strong again. She took a deep breath and tried to get herself back together again. The journey was important now. It was her grandmother's wish - her last wish. She must have had it on her mind for years. Had she only been waiting for Mary Rose to turn eighteen? It felt hard to believe that she was going on this mission, but she would. She would do, what her grandmother asked her to. Would she succeed?

She was scared, she did not know what it meant to be out on her own. Every time her grandmother had told her her story, she had been wondering, how she could survive, how she could go on. But then she knew the answer: it was Fortune.

Mary Rose started her preparations right away. She wanted to complete the mission whilst her grandmother was still alive. She knew how much it meant to her. She also knew that her grandmother was very old, and she did not know, how much time she had left on Earth. So she did not want to lose any time. As soon as the weather was warmer and less stormy, she wanted to set out on her mission. Maybe in April she would start the journey. For her, it was very clear how she would travel: by horse. This journey was more than just bringing something back to repay a debt; it was at the heart of her grandmother's life. The completion of this mission entangled her own life ever closer with her grandmother's. And it would connect present and past, her life with the life of that special woman, Scotland and the whole of

Europe, fate and fortune, destiny and purpose, humans and horses.

At stake was everything her grandmother believed in. She herself had met the kindest creatures in the moment of her greatest need, in the face of death, on the flight from evil. That woman had shown her kindness, bravery and courage and had given her the most precious gift she had ever received in her life. It had saved her so many times. This was the reason why she still believed in the good in people and in the world - even after all she had gone through. And that, Mary Rose knew, was one of the most precious things on Earth. And it was her mission to return the favour to the woman who had saved her grandmother with this gift.

"If you receive blessings, you give blessings," her grandmother had always said to her. "Save the faith in the good of this world," she had said every so often.

Now Mary Rose saw suddenly the whole picture. Her grandmother's life was a mosaic and she needed to put the final piece in place to make it a complete picture. It would be wonderful when it was finished. This piece was missing. It was an important piece for the final picture. Mary Rose understood the importance of this mission. That was why she had been chosen. Because she knew.

THE SAGA

*W*hen Rosmarie was a child, her grandmother told her a story of a unicorn that lived in the mountains of the Austrian Alps, in forests of the highland valley just above the alpine cabin where her grandparents spent the summers. This story became Rosmarie's favourite story, and she would beg her grandmother to tell it to her again and again. Rosmarie loved the story. Even today, in January 2001, when Rosmarie was about to turn eighteen, she remembered those days fondly. She revelled in memories. As a child she spent the summers with her grandparents in their cabin in the Austrian Alps. She remembered how her grandmother used to bring her to bed sitting down by the side of her bed, and Rosmarie would beg her grandmother to tell her a bedtime story. She loved stories, and she loved grandmother's stories most of all. They were always about good witches, unicorns and brave young women.

"Granny, can you tell me the story of the unicorn and the woman again?" Rosmarie asked her grandmother when she brought her to bed.

"Alright, my darling, but afterwards you wander straight to dreamlands," her grandmother Frieda replied.

"I promise!"

"Once upon a time, in the dense forests in the mountains, magical creatures populated the woodlands. The most wonderful of all was a unicorn. At first sight, it looked like a graceful horse. But, visible only to some humans, who do not see with their eyes only, but with their heart - this horse had a crystal sparkle around its head. It had a transparent, almost invisible horn on its forehead. This horn was formed of the light of love. There were many legends about the unicorn in all of the mountain valleys, and people talked about it all over the mountains and valleys, but hardly anybody had ever seen the unicorn. Your great-great-grandmother Susanna however, was one of the very few people who had! One day in late August Susanna was high up in the mountains. Just like us, your grandfather and myself, they were mountain farmers. On this day Susanna had been worrying, that a cold storm would come over the alpine pastures far earlier than usual. The family's herd of cows was still up there on the highland pastures, just underneath the Towers - the highest peaks of the highland valley. She feared that the cows would get killed in the storm. She knew it was dangerous to go out there now, but she needed to save the cows - they were all the family had. She hurried up to the grazing land as fast as she could. She called her cows and herded them down towards the shed on the lower highland pastures, halfway to the valley. But it was too late, and the snow storm swept over the highland pastures. Susanna and her herd got caught by the icy wind, that blew snow horizontally across the landscape. The wind was lashing, and she could not see anything in the snow storm. She made it to the forest with her herd, and drove them further downwards towards the cowshed. Suddenly, the fog thickened amongst the trees of the forest. Soon, the fog was so thick and white that she could not see anything anymore. The snow fell in big flakes covering the ground and making everything white. The snowy ground and the foggy air - whiteness all around her. She stumbled through the forest with her cows and lost all sense of direction. Then the cows stopped and refused to move on. They turned around and they went in the opposite direction to where Susanna tried to drive them. Suddenly she realised that she was standing right at the edge of the ravine. Another step, and she would have fallen into the depths of the ravine, crashed onto the rocks below and been washed away by the thunderous mountain river. She froze, paralysed by fear. The fog was so thick, she could barely see beyond her nose. She knew, it was dangerous to move. The wind was so cold, she felt frozen. The ice storm howled mercilessly. So she stood there, unable to move, unable to think. Fear crawled into her bones with the cold of the snowstorm. The fog obscured her vision and the wind numbed her brain. She fought a creeping desire to just sit down and wait for death. Then, suddenly, all the cows lifted their heads and seemed to be staring in the same direction. Susanna saw an icicle that sparkled with a crystal light, just for a second, before it vanished again. She stared into the thick fog and suddenly she saw a shadowy figure of a horse in the fog. It seemed to look in her direction, but then turned and walked away. The cows started walking too, all at once, as if to a command that Susanna couldn't hear. She followed the cows. She was so cold, she could hardly walk. She felt like she was being frozen, while still alive somehow. Two of her oldest cows stopped and waited for her. They shielded her from the wind and the snow to her right and to her left. Susanna was surprised, and somehow touched. She had never thought that her cows would protect her. It touched her deeply. A sensation warmed her for a moment - it was a feeling of love that was flowing through her. Then, after a while, she could not say how long, she saw the outline of a shed in the fog. She could scarcely believe her eyes: the unicorn and the cows had led her to a stable. They had saved her! She pulled the door open and squeezed all her cows into the tiny shed. When she turned around to look for the unicorn, she saw a shadow disappearing in the fog and the snowstorm."

"How lucky that the unicorn came to save Susanna!" Rosmarie exclaimed.

"Yes, indeed, she was very lucky. But it was not just luck, I believe. Because in the same snow storm a farmer, a hunter and a woodcutter died. An old legend tells that unicorns bring good luck only to those people who have a good heart."

Rosmarie remembered how she listened to her grandmother in awe. Back then she decided that she wanted to have a good heart. She loved unicorns. Maybe, one day a unicorn would bring good luck to her too?

"Tell me more about unicorns, grandma," she asked her grandmother. Her grandmother seemed to know everything about them.

"A unicorn is a horse, but a special one. It is believed to have a unique sparkle. And it is said to carry the light of love. But only people who are honest and kind-hearted can recognise that it is a unicorn. Other people might just see a horse. And here, in the Alps of Austria, people tell the saga of the unicorn that lives up there in the forests and watches over the life in the forests, the mountains, the rivers and meadows. It is kind to the kind. But it has no mercy for those who are not compassionate towards other living beings. The hunter that died that night, died close to the shed to which the unicorn led our great-great-grandmother. I believe that the unicorn saved her because she had a kind heart. It was not just luck. And also, maybe, the old stone-hearted hunter would not even have had the thought to follow a mirage in the fog."

Frieda paused for a moment to let her granddaughter think about that. When she finally nodded, she kissed her granddaughter on her forehead.

"You are a wonderful young lady. Keep your heart honest and kind. Then the unicorn might come to save you, when your are in great need."

Rosmarie nodded. "I will."

Frieda smiled at her granddaughter. "Good night, sweet dreams, sleep tight."

"Good night!" Rosmarie snuggled up in her bed and closed her eyes. She had a gentle smile on her face as she fell asleep.

OF KNIGHTS AND UNICORNS

*M*ary Rose was staring at the letter that her grandmother had given her. Printed on the envelope was the family's clan coat of arms: a shield escutcheon with a unicorn. Mary Rose took the envelope. Her fingers moved smoothly over the surface and touched the emblem. She remembered asking her grandfather about the unicorn emblem when she was a child. Now seeing it once more was like being spirited into the past. She liked to remember the days of her childhood. Somehow those were wonderful, almost magical memories. Her grandmother had always told her stories of unicorns. And her grandfather had told her stories of knights and unicorns.

"Grandpa, why is there a unicorn on the flag?" Mary Rose once asked her grandfather.

"The unicorn is a symbol of liberty and power. It is the symbol of Scotland. And it is the symbol of our family's clan," her grandfather explained.

Mary Rose was amazed. "So why is the unicorn the symbol of our family?"

"Because we are descendants of a family of knights. Our ancestors were knights. Knights were horsemen. They were warlords and they fought by horse. And every clan had an emblem. We have the unicorn. It is a great symbol to have. The unicorn is special. It is said to have special powers. Some say, it has even magical powers," grandfather Graham explained and leaned back in his wing chair. He let the words settle for a while and then he added:

"And if you think of it, that makes our family a house of knights of the unicorns."

Mary Rose thought about that for a while. Then she finally asked:

"Have there really been unicorns? Where did they go?"

"Well, some legends tell that there were a few of these magical creatures around, in deep forests all over Europe, but humans hunted them for the magic properties of their blood and their horn. They were all killed and now they are extinct. Not one unicorn is left," grandfather Graham said.

Mary Rose was sad to hear that. She felt sorry for the unicorns that were hunted and killed, and it made her sad. Just a moment earlier she had learned that she was a descendant from a house of knights of the unicorn. But who was a knight of the unicorn without a unicorn?

"But, there are other stories too," grandmother Annemarie threw in.

Mary Rose's face lit up a little bit. "Tell me!"

Grandmother Annemarie lowered her voice and whispered as if she was telling a secret:

"Some stories tell that the unicorn was a magical creature, like a horse, but a very special, strong and magical horse. Some sagas tell that a unicorn looks like an ordinary horse to normal people. It is a magical animal, but only those who believe in it can see it."

"So knights can see them?" Mary Rose asked.

"Oh well, I guess only some of them. The good ones," grandfather Graham replied. "Only those who are magnanimous, noble-minded and good-natured."

Mary Rose thought about that for a while.

"A wide-spread legend of the unicorn tells that unicorns are wild creatures that freely roam the forest. And they only come to women who are pure. The priests say it means they only come to virgins. But that is a misinterpretation. The unicorns come only to those who are pure-hearted," grandmother Annemarie continued.

Grandfather Graham agreed and he added: "We as horse-people know one thing for sure: horses come only to people who are good-hearted and sincere. Hence, if the unicorn is horse-like, it will only come to those who have a good heart, character and attitude." He paused for a moment before he continued to speak.

"And if you remember everything I taught you about knights, then you know that becoming a knight is about forming a person's character most of all."

Mary Rose looked at him with her eyes wide open and nodded. "Yes, grandpa, I remember."

"And if you remember what I taught you about Horsemanship, then you know that being a horseman -

or a horsewoman - is about forming a person's character in the first place."

Mary Rose nodded again. "Yes, grandpa, I remember."

"Whether you are a knight or a horseman, make sure you form your character. And horses are the best trainers for that."

"So knights and horsemen can see unicorns?" Mary Rose asked.

Grandmother Annemarie looked at her granddaughter with a conspiring wink and said:

"Do you know what I think?"

"What?" Mary Rose said breathless. She was so curious to hear what her wise Grandmother was going to tell her.

"I think they are just horses. I think the unicorn is a metaphor for the magic of horses. There are horses that are so beautiful, generous and graceful, so strong, enduring and fast, so true, devoted and faithful, so brave, superior and sensitive, that it is unbelievable. The horse is a creature so miraculous that it seems magical to us humans. When we humans encounter such a horse, we are awestruck, we cannot believe that all these qualities, can be embodied in one creature: in a horse."

Mary Rose nodded. "Yes, that is true. Horses are magical to me."

"Exactly, and I believe that is the source of the legends of the unicorns," her grandmother continued. "Throughout Europe and all over the world, the unicorn recurs in legends. Legends are said to have a true source, but often the truth is disguised and one needs to interpret metaphors, analogies and parables. The true core of the legends of the unicorn is the horse. I think it is just a metaphor for those special horses, that are too good to be true, too magical to be real and too extraordinary to be ordinary horses."

Grandmother Annemarie paused for a moment before she added:

"My horse itself was such a horse."

Mary Rose agreed. "Yes, you are right! Your horse was a magic horse. And so are her foals. And only us believers know that. We have our own unicorns."

Grandmother Annemarie smiled and said: "Yes, they are our unicorns."

Ever since this conversation with her grandparents as a child they had called their horses unicorns. All three of them were descendants of her grandmother's horse - the magic horse that had saved her grandmother's life.

Mary Rose did not know how often she asked her grandmother to tell her the story of her encounter with her horse. It must have been almost a hundred times that her grandmother told her the story of the brave horse that had saved her grandmother's life. Of all the magical stories of unicorns, the true story of her grandmother and her horse was the greatest for Mary Rose.

THE CURSE

*I*t was a great disappointment for Rosmarie. It was her eighteenth birthday and once again, she did not get what she had wished for her entire life. Since she was six years old, she had wished for nothing but a horse. She never got one. But she had been smart, and because she knew she might never get a horse from her parents, nor her grandparents, she had always wished for money instead. She had saved every single cent, and on top of that, she had worked hard. Every holiday, she had worked as a waitress and earned her own money. Now she had almost enough money to buy herself a horse. She would make her dream come true. She was an adult woman now, and she did not need to rely on her parents and grandparents to fulfill her greatest wish.

She took the envelope with money, packed her belongings and left the family apartment. She went to the bank and paid the money into her account. Then she stood in the street, took a deep breath and started walking. Her home town was a small town in the Austrian Alps, small, but quite pretty. As she walked past the town-hall, she noticed the flag of the town that was blowing in the wind. It showed a black unicorn. She stopped for a moment and admired it. The unicorn had always fascinated her. It seemed to be everywhere in the mountain towns and villages, as an emblem on flags and coats of arms, pubs and hotels were named after it, and even companies used it as their company logo. Then she remembered, she had a train to catch and started walking again. It was the first day of the semester holiday and Rosmarie was going to work. She went to the station to catch the train towards the mountain valley. Once she arrived in the valley, she caught a bus that took her further up towards the mountains. Eventually, she hopped off the bus at her grandparents' home.

She could see the two hundred year old farm house at the bottom of a hill. It was an idyllic sight. The house was surrounded by meadows which had been green in spring, but were now buried beneath a blanket of snow. Majestic, aged trees lined along the long path towards the house. Rosmarie walked past the old chestnut trees and the pond. She crossed the torrent and then she saw the cows in front of the shed, puffing out steaming fog clouds into the cold air. When she got closer, Rolf, her grandmother's wolf-dog barked in greeting and then started trotting towards her, tail wagging. Rosmarie hugged the dog and they walked together towards the house. Her grandmother, alerted by the sound of the dog, appeared in the doorway. Rosmarie ran up and embraced her.

"Oh Rosmarie, how nice you have come to see us! Come in!" Frieda was delighted to see her granddaughter.

Rosmarie smiled and followed her grandmother along the creaking wooden floorboard, past a wall with the cowbells and all the prizes the family's cows had won. They entered the small, wood-panelled living room. The tiled stove spread a cosy warmth and it smelled of wood. They sat down at the old, hand-carved table in the middle of the room.

"Are you on your way to the alpine hut? When are you going to start work," grandmother Frieda wanted to know.

"Tomorrow. I can go there this afternoon or early in the morning," Rosmarie answered.

"You can stay with us, darling Rosmarie. And tomorrow in the morning, your uncle is going up to the highlands to check if the roofs of the cow shed and the hut have withstood the snow. He can take you up there."

Rosmarie agreed. She liked being with her grandmother Frieda, though she sometimes was annoyed by her grumpy old grandfather, Viktor. Her parents had no contact with him, following a feud with her other grandfather, Erhard. Once Viktor had forbidden his daughter to have any relationship with this family. Her mother Viktoria had defiantly married her father Engelbert anyway - very much to the chagrin of Viktor. Rosmarie sometimes was annoyed with him for being so hardened and obstinate. But she couldn't change that, so she had to come to accept it.

"Here, this is for your birthday, my darling," Frieda said.

"Thank you!" Rosmarie took the envelope and opened it. Her eyes widened. "Wow! That is a lot of money! I can't take so much from you."

"Oh yes, you will need it to feed your horse."

Rosmarie was baffled. "How do you know?"

"My dear Rosmarie, I am your grandmother. I just know about your deepest wish."

Rosmarie had tears in her eyes as she fell into her grandmother's arms. They held each other for a while.

"You know? But why don't my parents know? And why don't they allow me to have a horse? Why don't they even allow me to go horse-riding?"

"Oh, dear Rosmarie, they love you very much. They are just scared that something might happen to you."

"Why would something happen to me? I mean, I want a horse, not a dragon."

Frieda sighed deeply. "Well, it is because your grandfather believes that a horse is to blame for the death of his first fiancée. He thinks that these wonderful creatures are cursed. And he had always told your mother that it is dangerous to keep a horse, and that she needs to stay away from these creatures. Your mother heard that often. When she was a child, she also was fascinated by horses, but her grandfather never allowed her to start riding."

Rosmarie's mouth stood wide open. Then she gasped out:

"What? You never told me this! I didn't even know, that grandfather Viktor had a fiancée before you. What happened? Tell me everything! I want to know."

Frieda remained quiet for a while, as if in deep thought. After a long and awkward silence, she said:

"Maybe I shouldn't have told you. Your grandfather never talks about it. And he hates it when I dig up old stories that he wants to forget. I think, he never spoke to anyone about it - not me, not your mother, nobody. He would not want me to tell you."

She paused for a moment before she added:

"But I think, you should know."

She paused for another long while, before she continued:

"I myself do not know what happened exactly. It was before my time here. Victor always said: 'Let the past be the past,' when I asked him about it. But I do know that the family had a beautiful horse - a white horse - just like the unicorn on the family's emblem. And I know that your grandfather believes that it was this horse's fault that his first fiancée died during the war. He did once tell me the horse was cursed. But I think the war is the curse, not the horse. The war destroyed so many lives. And it divided the people - the war is the cause of the feuds between family clans."

"Hold on," Rosmarie said abruptly, trying to compose all of this new information in her head.

"I did not even know, we have an emblem. One with a unicorn on it? Can I see it?"

Frieda stood up and walked towards the door where she stopped and beckoned Rosmarie over.

"Come, I'll show you something."

THE DIARY

*M*ary Rose wanted to make the same journey her grandmother once had, but in the opposite direction, from Scotland to Austria. Therefore, she decided to start reading her grandmother's travel diary from back to front, studying the passages that her grandmother had written in the same places the events took place. This way Mary Rose could experience her grandmother's journey in the most intimate way. On some days she could hardly wait to start riding. On other days, she was scared and worried.

That evening it was stormy again and the rain was lashing against the windows of the cottage. Mary Rose stood at the window and watched the storm blowing across the landscape. She could see the sea on the horizon, and through the rain she could make out the sight of waves breaking against the cliffs and splashing high into the sky. Mary Rose was glad to be safe and warm inside the cottage. Even the horses, hardy from a life out in the elements, were inside in the shed instead of grazing on the pastures. She ventured out to the shed, to make sure the horses had everything they needed. They were chewing their hay and just paused and looked at her for a moment when she entered the shed. They seemed to be comfortable. She stroked the neck of each of the three horses and kissed them good night. Then she ran back to the cottage in the rain.

Inside the cottage it was cosy and warm. It smelled of cinnamon and baked apples from the apple pie she had put in the oven. The fire was crackling. She made a cup of herbal tea for her grandmother and one for herself and then cuddled up on the sofa with her grandmother's travel diary. It was an old book bound in leather. It had the typical smell of old books. The few pages were hand-sewed and very worn out. Mary Rose touched it with awe and respect. She opened it and started reading the last chapter.

I still have no idea where I am going. Where should I go? I have lost my home and my family. The only one I have is this horse. And because she only brought good fortune to me, I decided to put my life into her hands - well, hoofs. I was too tired to think and too hopeless to plan. So I just sat on her back and let her walk where she wanted.

She kept walking along the wild coasts of Great Britain. Here, close to the coast she could always find some grass and herbs. And there weren't that many people. Every time we encounter people, I can see them watching the horse in awe. Everybody, men, women, children alike, the moment they spot the white horse, they cannot take their eyes off it. It is just exactly how I feel.

Since the horse is leading, we just wander along the coast. Every now and then, we pause and she starts grazing for a while. I also go and look for food. I found some berries, some herbs and roots, some mushrooms. Then we start walking again. We never stay somewhere for too long. We are always on the move, but she never hurries.

After several weeks the horse walked onto a very beautiful stretch of land on the coast. The horse slowed down and I got off her back. We strolled through the landscape looking for food.

And then, suddenly, I saw a horse coming towards us. It was a tall brown horse with a man on it. I could not believe my eyes. I rubbed them and looked again. A good looking man on a horse came towards me. I stood there and I stared at him. I was somehow unable to run away. But also the white horse stood there and watched them coming closer, so I did the same.

Then he stopped right in front of me. His horse was tall. Taller than mine and thinner. It must be a thoroughbred, I thought. Then he said something, but I did not get what he said. He realised that I didn't understand, and then he spoke in well pronounced English that I understood. He said:

"Welcome to Scotland. This is my family's land. Can I help you?"

I just stood there and looked at the handsome man.

"I... I...," I stuttered.

Then the white horse gave me a nudge. I pulled myself together, took a deep breath and spoke with my very best English:

"Sir, thank you, that is very kind of you. We are refugees, we have no home and we are hungry. Please, if you would be so kind to allow my horse to graze on your *meadows and drink from your river, that would be very kind."*

He said: "You are welcome. Come with me." He turned his horse and started riding.

I looked at the white horse and it nodded. So I hopped on her back and we followed him. We rode over a hill and from the top we had an even better view. Oh how beautiful this scenery was! I had never seen anything like this before. The river wound through the headland towards a manor. At the horizon was the sea and the sky. It was the most beautiful piece of land I had seen since I had left home. He pointed at the manor and said:

"My grandfather lives there."

I was very impressed. We continued riding and I tried not to stare at him. We rode past a herd of sheep and over another hilltop and then we saw a cottage nearby a lake. He smiled at me and said:

"This is my place."

I smiled back. I could not believe my luck. Was he taking me to his home? Was he going to give me something to eat? Was he going to give me shelter for the night? I was praying that he would offer me somewhere to stay. I was so tired and exhausted, and even though I had started to get used to the horse's way of life, I was craving a bed, a bath and a cup of hot tea. All of which I had not had in a long time. Suddenly I realised how dirty I must be. I felt embarrassed, because the man was well-dressed and clean.

Soon, he stopped in front of the cottage. Besides the cottage were two sheds, and we brought the horses into the one closest to the house. He gave my horse water, hay and oats. She let him touch her neck, and she proudly lifted her head up when he said:

27

"That is a truly beautiful horse."

I decided then to trust this man, because the white horse seemed to trust him and I knew I could rely on her instincts. And I wanted so much, to be able to trust someone, more than I was longing for a bed, a bath and a tea. Someone human, that is. I knew I was lucky to have the white horse to trust, but it had been so long since another human had noticed me, cared for me and respected me.

So I followed him to his cottage. It was cosy inside. He lit a fire and the room warmed quickly. He heated water for a bath for me and he made me tea! After the bath, I came to sit down at the fire. He gave me a bowl of oats soaked in hot water with salt. I had not eaten something that delicious in a long time. Then he looked at me and said with a gentle smile:

"You and your horse, you can stay as long as you want."

In that moment, a huge tear welled in my eye and rolled across my cheeks. The first tear I had cried in a long time was a tear of happiness.

Mary Rose put the book down. So that was how her grandmother met her grandfather. She sat on the sofa and watched the storm for a while and let the story settle. It was a wonderful story, she thought. They were happy together. Until grandfather Graham died one night. He just fell asleep and never woke up again. Grandmother Annemarie had lost a lot of her will to live when her husband died. Mary Rose noticed that straight away. That was why she decided to live with her grandmother, because she needed somebody who was there for her. At the same time Mary Rose herself preferred living in Scotland to life in London where her parents had an apartment. So it was good for both of them.

Grandmother Annemarie slept in the rocking chair at the fireplace. Mary Rose stood up, and she put out the fire. She woke her grandmother up and helped her into bed and said good night to her. Then she went to bed herself and fell asleep straight away.

THE EMBLEM

*R*osmarie followed her grandmother up the creaking wooden stairs to the top of the old farm house. It was a slow climb, as her grandmother found it more and more difficult to take the steps up to the top floor. Finally they arrived at the top, and Frieda opened the door to the room just underneath the roof. It was a kind of bureau with a bookcase, a big secretaire desk and a fire place. Rosmarie had never been in this room. It was her grandfather's office, and she had not been allowed to go in there when she was a child. To the right side, she noticed a flag on the wall showing a white unicorn.

Frieda walked up to it and said: "This is our family's emblem. As you can see, it is a unicorn. The unicorn stands for power and liberty, wisdom and honesty. Once, your grandfather and his ancestors were very proud of this coat of arms. Your great-great-grandfather Friedrich was the only farmer in all of the five valleys to be rewarded with a coat of arms. He was the only farmer who had been awarded the privileges and the rights of knights. And he was known throughout the valleys of the Austrian Alps."

Frieda paused for a moment. Rosmarie inspected the flag thoroughly. Then she turned around and looked expectantly at her grandmother. Frieda started telling the story:

"One day, Friedrich had been working in the fields far up in the mountains and was making his way home when it started to get dark. He walked downwards along the stream and along the ravine. When he came to the rapids and the waterfall he suddenly saw a white horse. He thought that it might be the unicorn that had saved his wife once, so he walked up to it. However, it was a horse with a saddle but without a rider. The horse was nervous and thus he thought that something might have happened. So he started to look for the rider and he found a man that had fallen into the ravine. He was still alive, lying unconsciously in the ice cold water of the mountain river. Friedrich pulled him out with the help of a rope and the horse and he put him over the horse's back. He then brought the man to his cabin further down the highland valley. He and his wife Susanna nursed the man back to health. When he recovered, he thanked them many times and eventually rode off. Half a year later, the man returned with two beautiful white horses. He turned out to be a lord and he gave one white horse to Friedrich and Susanna, as well as this coat of arms. Friedrich had gained the lord's favour and he was known as the Knightly Farmer all across the country."

Rosmarie listened to the story with awe. So little she had known. Why had nobody ever told her this story?

"The family was known throughout the country, and wherever Friedrich went out on the back of his beautiful horse, everybody showed him great respect. He became the mayor of the village and the family was blessed."

Frieda paused and then she whispered conspiratorially: "The family's emblem protects a secret. You must keep it to yourself and not tell anybody - except your children, one day when they are ready."

Rosmarie nodded and whispered back: "I will not tell anybody. The secret of the family's emblem is safe with me."

Frieda pulled at the wooden stick at the top of the flag with the unicorn emblem. She took it off the wall and revealed a spear at the end of the stick. She pushed the spearhead into a knothole in the wooden panel. It disappeared into the hole and she turned it until it made a clicking noise. She turned the spear back again: another click. As she turned it back a third time the panel opened and revealed a dark corridor.

Frieda went inside and lit a torch. Rosmarie followed. Frieda closed the door carefully behind them.

"Behind the chimney is a very small staircase which leads to the secret chamber underneath the roof and the tunnel ahead of us is a secret exit."

Rosmarie just could not believe what she was seeing. There was a secret tunnel in her grandparents' house and she had never known about it.

"What is this tunnel for, grandmother?"

"Well, it saved lives. You know, times were rough.

There was a time when neighbouring tribes fell into our valley and stole cattle and women. There was a time when women were burnt if they had red hair, were independent-minded or knew about healing herbs. A woman of your grandfather's family clan was a midwife, and one day a mother died in childbirth and she could not save her and then she was accused of witchcraft. She escaped through this secret tunnel. As the family saga says, she lived out her days in a secret place in the mountains. She lived a long and happy life after all. And there were times when war came all the way into the valley, people were hunted and deported for their political view, their religious beliefs, their ethnic origin or even for whom they loved. In times like those such a tunnel could really be life-saving."

They climbed the staircase and entered a room with low ceiling, just underneath the roof. It was too small for either of them to stand upright. To the left was a mattress; to the right was a safe and an antique-looking chest.

"Here we keep the treasures of the family."

Frieda opened the safe. She whispered the code into Rosmarie's ear. Rosmarie nodded. Frieda handed her a golden medal. The unicorn was engraved in it.

"This is what Friedrich got from the lord. The medal, the flag and a scroll that entitled our family to special rights - and the horse."

Frieda showed the scroll to Rosmarie.

Rosmarie was awestruck to hear that her family had a coat of arms. And on top of that it was not just any emblem, with an eagle or a lion or an ibex, but with the unicorn. The unicorn was the family's heraldic beast. Rosmarie felt like she suddenly understood a part of herself, of her past, of her ancestors. It felt like she had just found a lost part of herself, a missing piece in her puzzle. She had always felt a bit strange, lacking a sense of belonging to her family. She had always liked her grandmother, but never found a connection to her grandfather. It had hardly helped that her parents had stopped speaking to him after he refused to give his blessing for their marriage. The dispute had deeply disrupted the family. Frieda seemed to be constantly trying to balance the grimness of grandfather Victor, but the gap in the family remained. Rosmarie sometimes resented her grandfather - and to a certain extent her parents - for their inability to leave the dispute behind. As such she had always missed that feeling of belonging to a family clan, to her ancestors and to a history beyond her parents' marriage.

Having learned about her great-great-grandfather Friedrich, she felt deep respect for this man she had never met. And for the first time in her life she wanted to learn about her ancestors and about the history of her family. For the first time she felt that she wanted to be part of this family, of this special clan with its distinctive emblem. She wanted to know more and unravel all the hidden secrets of the family.

In that moment, Frieda took an old book from the chest and showed it to Rosmarie. Rosmarie remembered the book: her grandmother had shown it to her, when she was a young girl.

"In this book, you will find all the information we have about our ancestors."

She opened the book carefully and leafed through it. When she found the page she was looking for she showed Rosmarie a picture of a tall and slim man and a white horse.

"This is Friedrich. He was a great man. It was his kindness and bravery that won the lord's favour and led to the award of the coat of arms. According to the records of the family, the lord said, the unicorns favour those that are kind and brave. Therefore the lord chose it as the heraldic beast for Friedrich. That was the greatest honour one could receive."

"And the horse?" Rosmarie asked. "Tell me more about the horse!"

Her grandmother put the book back in the chest and closed it. Then she continued to speak: "The family always kept horses. Generation after generation, until…"

Her grandmother paused and it seemed that her thoughts were taking her far back into the past.

"Until what?" Rosmarie said with growing impatience.

Frieda's expression darkened. Then she shook her head.

"That is another story, I will tell you another time."

"No, please tell me now, I want to know about the horses," Rosmarie begged her grandmother.

In that moment they heard heavy steps on the creaking floor downstairs.

"That is Victor. I have to look after him. Let's go back and hang up the flag."

"You can go back, grandma. I want to use the secret exit to see where it leads to."

Frieda nodded. They climbed down the ladder.

Frieda went out through the secret door in the wooden panels and handed Rosmarie the flashlight. Then the door closed.

KNIGHT OF THE UNICORN

*M*ary Rose was in deep thought when she put her wellington boots and her coat on, and went outside. She took a deep breath of fresh air. Green fields lay in front of her. The wind was blowing across the harsh landscape. At the bottom of the hill the horses were grazing next to the sheep. Mary Rose loved this beautiful place. She felt that she belonged here. At the age of thirteen she had decided to stay here with her grandmother instead of living in London with her parents. Her parents disliked this decision very much, but back then they were busy arguing with each other over an affair of her father and they almost divorced that summer. Whilst her parents were fighting their marital dispute, Mary Rose spent the summer with her grandparents. Unfortunately, her grandfather died shortly after she moved in. It was a lot to take for Mary Rose, she suffered very much under the loss of her grandfather, and she needed to be in a peaceful place to recover.

When autumn came she refused to come back to London. She needed peace and wanted to be far away from her arguing parents. And she had always loved life in Scotland with her grandparents. She loved the horses. She loved the headland and the view of the sea and the sunset on the horizon. After her grandfather died, she felt that grandmother Annemarie really needed some company. So Mary Rose stayed.

She felt that her parents were hurt by her decision to reject their way of life in London in favour of the rural life with her grandparents in Scotland. Besides their arguing and her grandmother in need of support certainly the horses had played a major role in this decision. Her parents knew that she had never been really happy in London. She had never felt that she belonged there. She belonged here. That was where she wanted to be. In the midst of green hills, in a cottage with a view of the sea and the grazing horses. Her parents never understood it. Mary Rose's mother was impatient to leave for London when she was young, moving out when she was eighteen. She moved down to the capital and married a Londoner. But her daughter never became a real Londoner. Her heart was bound to the horses, the green hills, the sky and the sea.

'Maybe it would be a good idea to write a letter to my parents. That way, I'd be gone when they receive the letter and it will be too late for them to stop me,' Mary Rose thought.

She worried that they might not really understand what this journey was about. Her mother had always been afraid of horses and had never been able to experience the gifts that those creatures brought to a person who truly loved them. She had never been able to trust them. And so she never got a chance to sense what Mary Rose experienced when she was with the horses. Mary Rose felt sorry for her mother, because she had never been able to share this feeling that she loved more than anything.

She whistled gently, and the horses lift their heads and looked towards her. They started cantering in her direction, and stopped right in front of her. Mary Rose stroked their foreheads and their necks. She put a rope around the neck of one of them and asked it to kneel down, pointing at its foreleg. She sat on its back, and they went for a ride. The other two horses stayed close by and followed without a leash. She rode to the headland and took in the view of the sea. The water was sparkling in the rays of sunshine that came out between the fast moving clouds. Mist rose from the cliffs. The water was wide open and its only limit was the sky. The tide was low so she rode down to the beach.

The horses walked along the beach in a rhythmic walk. All of them walked in one line, shoulder by shoulder, head by head. The seagulls were flying past them and encouraged them to fly along the beach with them. The younger horse started to prance and threw its head up in a high-spirited gesture. It said it wanted to run. Mary Rose let her horse drop into a canter, and they started to run with the wind. It felt like the horses' hooves stopped touching the ground and they had started to fly. Mary Rose loved this feeling of sitting on the back of a flying horse. For her, it was absolute freedom and full trust at the same time. Only those who can trust their horse are able to experience something like this, she was certain.

At the end of the beach the horses slowed down. She turned, and they walked back through the shallow water. The surf washed around the horses' hooves. For Mary Rose this moment in time was just perfect. She was happy. The beach was beautiful. The sea touched the horses. The wind carried the ocean spray up through the air. She looked at the horizon where the sea met the sky. Back in the other direction were green hills, sheep and the cottage in the sun. She loved this place. She picked up a trail across the grassland, around the manor, and when she reached the top of the hill, she stopped.

This must have been the place where her grand-mother saw the cottage for the first time. No surprise that she fell in love with it straight away. It was such an idyllic landscape. Or maybe, she had fallen in love with her grandfather at first sight? Or maybe both - most likely, it might have been a bit of both.

'Funny,' Mary Rose thought, 'isn't it funny that the horse kept walking until it reached this hill? I wonder why. Was it meant to be? Did the horse know that this was its destiny? Why and how did they come all the way up here to Scotland? They just went on and on, day by day. Every day they walked a bit and in the end they came here and decided to stay. It is fascinating. It really is.'

Mary Rose got off the horse and sat down at the spot where she thought her grandmother had seen her future home for the very first time. She took an empty book from her bag. It was to be her new diary, her travel diary.

She thought, it would be good to start it here and now. So she sat down in the grass and started writing.

I have been knighted. On my eighteenth birthday, I have been knighted by my grandmother. She said I am a knight of the unicorn now. For me she is the real knight - a sorceress of the unicorns. I know nobody who is as good with horses as my grandmother.Not even my grandfather was as good as she is, and he was considered to be the best horseman in Scotland. My grandmother and the horses - that is special. When she talks to horses and dances with them, it looks like magic. With gentle, tiny, little gestures, she can make the horse stop and go, run off and come back, rear up and lie down. It does not matter if she is yards away. The horses listen to her and follow. One day, I want to be a horse whisperer as good as my grandmother.

But now, it is the time to see, I will see how good the bond between me and the horse really is. Will it follow me, even when we leave home? Will it stay with me, even when we are riding into an unknown future? I will see. I hope I can live up to my grandmother's perception of me. I wish I can live up to her expectations. I hope I can complete this journey and fulfill her wish. The burden feels heavy. And I feel too small to complete the task. But I must try and give my very best. Maybe - hopefully - my grandmother is right and I will prove to be as strong as she thinks I am.

The truth is, I am scared. I am scared of leaving home and grandma, I am scared of being out there alone. I am scared that the horse gets injured. I am scared of going on this journey, but more than this, I am scared of failing. And most of all I am scared of thinking that grandma might be leaving soon.

41

I remember grandpa always told me stories of knights and unicorns. He said that I will become a knight one day. He said I am strong, brave, kind and smart. That's what it takes. I wish he was here. He made me believe I am brave. He once told me, that after the basic education with a master every apprentice has to pass one's own unique exam that will be posed by life. I hope I will succeed prove being worthy.

Whenever I get scared of going on this journey just accompanied by my horse, I imagine myself as a knight on a unicorn's back: I have a shining light around me. It is my suit of armour that shows people my strength that is supplied by the light of pure loving energy. My weapon is love and my mission is to bring bliss. Then I recover my confidence and I start believing that I will be strong enough to complete this mission.

Mary Rose closed her diary. She felt better now. The ride with her horses helped her gain energy and strength again. And thinking of her grandfather helped her gain confidence. Her grandfather had always believed in her. He had never doubted that she would become a knight one day. So why did she doubt it? It was not a title for her grandfather, it was not an ancient right, it was an attitude, skills and character. Just as her grandfather always told her.

In this moment she realised that she had not trained her knightly skills at all since her grandfather's death. It made her sad when she did. The pain was so strong for a while that she just could not do it.

'I have to get back to training,' Mary Rose said to herself. 'I have to stop moaning and start training. Knightly skills are what I need. It will remind me how strong I really am. I will see what my grandparents see in me. I will start training tomorrow.'

Mary Rose got up and started walking. Now she felt determined. She had a plan. She knew what to do. She would plan her journey in detail and work on her knightly skills.

Mary Rose strolled towards the cottage that she called her home. She was deep in thought as she walked back, and it was only as she came closer that she realised that a big grey car parked in front of the cottage. She knew who that was.

THE WITCH AND THE UNICORN

*R*osmarie was left in the dark, overwhelmed by her feelings. She had to bend her head down to avoid the tunnel's ceilings. At the far end, a ladder led downwards. But before she climbed down to see where the tunnel led to, she climbed up for another look at the tiny room upstairs. Quietly, she opened the safe and the chest. She took the medallion and looked at it again. It really was a horse with a horn on its forehead. It also had a big dent in it. She put it back. Then she looked at the book of her ancestors again. She remembered that her grandmother Frieda had shown it to her when she was younger. It must have been when she was about thirteen.

That time Rosmarie had responded: "Grandma, I am not a horse, I don't need a family tree."

"It is about where you come from, and your ancestors. You should take an interest. Maybe you can learn something about yourself and your family," her grandmother had replied.

At that time, Rosmarie was not particularly interested in her ancestors, nor her family tree. But now, things were different. She wanted to know everything about Friedrich and the family's emblem. She would ask her grandmother to show her the book of her ancestors again! Maybe she could squeeze more stories out of her.

She started leafing through the book. There was a short paragraph about Friedrich. It told of how he had won the Lord's favour and received the family's coat of arms, as well as privileges, and a noble horse. But she could not find anything further about the horse itself. She put the book back carefully, closed the chest and the safe and looked around. Next to the mattress on the floor, a book lay in the dust. Rosmarie grabbed it. It was an old book with sagas from the region. She took it with her and started climbing down. It was a long descent, but finally she reached the floor. A cold shiver ran down her spine, thinking about how many lives this tunnel might have saved in the past. She thought of the women who were burnt for being independent, different-looking, or unwilling to fit into the template of a housewife and mother. She was shivering as she climbed into the cold darkness with thoughts as dark as these times.

Rosmarie herself was an emancipated woman. She liked to live her life as she pleased instead of satisfying other peoples' expectations. She was horrified to think that once young women like her were burnt on a pile of wood for no other reason than being independent-minded, red-haired or unconventional. She thought of herself and her female friends. All the women she got on well with were free-spirited. Her stomach turned when she thought how she and her friends could have been hunted, chained up and burned. Her whole body trembled, and she shook her head heavily. She wanted to get rid of these awful thoughts. She started to walk faster, and rushed through the tunnel as if she was chased by witch hunters. She could sense the fear of her ancestors who had escaped through the tunnel.

Then, suddenly, she found herself in front of a ladder, which rose up to a trapdoor. She climbed up and found she needed all her strength to open it. She could barely lift it up. After several exhausting attempts, she finally pushed it open. She found herself in the shed behind the house, where the firewood was stored. She closed the exit, silently left the shed, and returned to the old farmhouse.

Rosmarie wanted to ask her grandmother more about the secret chamber and the exit, about witches and unicorns, about the emblem and the history of the family. However her grandmother was just taking her grandfather outside to sit on the bench for a while. Her grandfather was very old, and even though he seemed in good shape, he needed help to negotiate the stairs. They sat down on the bench in front of the house and enjoyed the winter sun.

Rosmarie did not want to disturb them, so she went to her room and lay down on the bed. She took the book that she had found in the secret chamber and opened it. It was an old book with sagas from the mountain valleys of the Alps. Rosmarie started reading the first saga.

The witch and the unicorn

Once upon a time, high up in the mountains,
there was a witch living in the forest
amongst the deer, the foxes, the rabbits, the
birds and the trees. She was an evil witch
that cast spells on people, and sometimes she
guided people to their deaths in the ravine.
She polluted the water of the river. She grew
poisonous mushrooms and berries. She tried
to create thunderstorms and blizzards. She
ruled with brutal and merciless force in the
highlands of the mountains.

Many people were killed by her rage. So the
valley was known as a dangerous place, and
people avoided going there. Nobody knew
why her heart was so hardened, but there
was a rumour, that her parents died when
she was a baby, and that she had never
experienced love in her life. So her heart
was filled with fear in the cold and lonely
nights. She feared of humans so she went to
live in the mountains, all alone. Since fear
was what she carried in her heart, fear was
what she created. She used all her witchcraft
to create evil.

One day, the witch was walking through the
forest, and saw a bright light. She did not
like the light, just as she did not like the sun
either, so she summoned a big cloud to sit
right in front of the sun. But even as the
cloud cast its shadow, the bright light from
the wood persisted. She walked towards it,
wanting to find out where it came from. In

47

*a clearing in the forest she saw a white
horse, from which a bright light seemed to
shine, illuminating all around it. The witch
wanted to drive the horse away because she
did not like its light. So she lifted her wand,
and started to murmur an evil spell.*

*The horse lifted its head and looked at her.
From its forehead, the bright light shone
straight at the witch. And suddenly, she felt
the hardened stone shell of her heart
cracking, and for the first time in her life
she felt love.*

*From that day on, the witch changed. She
planted healing herbs all over the highlands,
and she purified the water. And over the
years, the cursed valley turned into one of
the most fruitful highlands of the Alps.
People came there to eat the herbs and drink
the water, believing them to have healing
properties, preserving good health and
giving a long life.*

Rosmarie put the book down and let her thoughts
stroll. The unicorn was everywhere here in the valleys.
She wondered what that meant. Somehow, she sensed
that the unicorn had a secret message for her. But what
was it saying? She needed to follow its call and follow its
traces. She needed to put the pieces of the stories
together and solve the puzzle. The unicorn appeared to
her again and again. But its appearance was fleeting - as
if it allowed just a glimpse before it disappeared again
into the depths of the forests.

PURPOSE AND PUZZLE

*W*hen Mary Rose arrived at the cottage, she recognised her parents' car. Her parents had come here? They had not been up here for a while. She took the rope off the horses' necks and quickly checked their hooves and legs. Then she released them onto the pasture. She went inside the house. Her parents and her grandmother were sitting in the living room, sipping tea and making polite conversation. Her mother Annabelle got up when she saw her daughter. She came towards Mary Rose and gave her a hug. Her father James did the same.

"Darling Mary Rose!", Annabelle said. "We thought, we'd make for a surprise visit for your birthday. I cannot believe that you are a grown woman now!"

James then handed her an envelope. "A birthday present," he said.

Mary Rose thanked them and opened the envelope. It was a cheque to cover her tuition fees at university. It came with a card saying that they only wanted the best for her, so they would cover her university fees at one of the best British universities - the one of her choice. Mary Rose had mixed feelings about the present. It was incredibly generous, but at the same time, she could not help feeling that it was another attempt of her parents to push her down a path - the path that they thought was the right one, not the one that Mary Rose thought was the best for her. It then made Mary Rose a bit angry and sad. Why did her parents never ever ask her what she wanted? How could they think they knew what was best for her without even bothering getting to know her?

She took a deep breath. She did not want to discuss her future plans with her parents now. So she smiled and thanked them very much for their generosity. But then her mother started fantasising, about how wonderful her life would be when she went to Oxford - or Cambridge - or maybe St. Andrews University. Mary Rose just couldn't listen to them anymore. She had other plans. And one day, her parents would have to learn this.

So she said: "I have thought about this long and hard and from all different angles," she started.

Suddenly her mother was quiet, staring right at her.

Mary Rose took a deep breath and spoke clearly, and with a strong voice:

"I have decided to take some time off."

"What?" Her parents said simultaneously and stared at her, dumbfounded.

"I have made plans. I want to see Europe, travel and think about what I really want. I have saved money from teaching horsemanship with grandpa and I can cover my expenses. When I come back, I might study."

"Darling, you can travel the whole summer. Then you would be ready to start studying in October. Don't lose more time, you might regret it later. Then you'll be older than all the others and it might be a little weird."

"I need to know my purpose before I make a choice."

"Darling, you will study law, as we have always planned. Since you were a child, we had this plan for you."

"Yes, you made plans for me, but you have never even bothered to ask me what I wanted. I did not want to go to the private school you sent me to either!"

Mary Rose was upset. She hated that her parents planned her life without her. It was her life!

Her parents looked at each other bewildered.

"You will find out about your purpose at some point in your life for sure. But you don't need to go travelling for that. You have to get on with your life and it will reveal itself."

"I am getting on with my life."

Her parents seemed to be helpless in a baffled way. Eventually James asked: "So what do you want, my dear?"

"I just told you. I want to take some time off, travel, find myself and my purpose, and then make the choice that is right for me."

Her parents exchanged a worried look in silence. Her grandmother was silent too, but looked at her with pride.

Mary Rose knew her parents. Apparently they had not changed at all. It seemed she would be forced to make herself very clear.

"I have decided already. I am a grown woman now, as

you've already mentioned, and I make my own decisions in my own life. I ask you to respect that. I am going on a journey. I will let you know about further plans."

Mary Rose got up and went outside. She knew this was typical of her parents, something that annoyed her no less after all these years. They had never understood her, but she felt that they had never even tried. She walked towards the three white horses that were grazing out in the green pasture. The horses lifted their heads when she came closer. She sat down next to them and took out her diary. She continued writing.

I have decided that my calling might be to become a knight of the unicorn - whatever that might mean in the end. I have had the thought that I am destined for this mission of bringing back the fortune of the unicorn to the woman who gave it to my grandmother. I was chosen to fulfil my grandmother's last wish. It is the missing piece in the puzzle of my grandmother's life. But at the same time by completing it, it will become a central piece in the puzzle of my own life.

For a while I felt lost in grief after my grandfather's death. I forgot about the things my grandfather taught me. I forgot who I was capable of becoming. I stopped training. I have not been at a single horse-show since my grandfather died. I stopped teaching humans and training horses, I stopped working with clients. Maybe I lost myself for a while. It looks like I cannot find a piece that fits into the puzzle at the moment. So maybe I need to look for a new one. And I think it is this same part of the puzzle that my grandmother needs as well. It is not just her puzzle, now it is also mine.

It already helped me to get back on track. It reminded me.

I might grow strong through this mission and be ready to stand on my own feet and walk the path into my future.

It makes me feel sad that I cannot make my parents understand why this is important for me. My parents don't feel the magic of horses. They don't feel the bliss that comes from being with them.

For me and for grandmother Annemarie, there is this invisible, yet sparkling bliss all around these horses. It is this bliss that saved her from getting lost in dark thoughts. The bliss of the horses helped her escape. It made her endure difficult times. It helped her to finally find a home, a man and love again.

I can feel this bliss. I can understand. And it is the same bliss that made me run away from the school my parents sent me to and that led me to the decision to stay here where I belong. I trust that this bliss, which guarded and guided my grandmother, will do the same for me.

I will find my purpose in the course of this journey.

Mary Rose closed her diary. It felt good to write a diary. She liked how she could fill the empty pages with her own words. She observed the grazing horses for a while. She remembered how she sat on this meadow as a child and her grandfather explained to her the body language of horses. Graham taught her to read every sign, every move of an eye, an ear, the tail, a step forward or the position of each horse in relation to the others. One of her most precious memories was the moment when Graham put his hat on her head after asking her questions about the relationship of the horses to each other and what she thought they were saying. He was obviously content with Mary Rose's answers and he said approvingly:

"Well done, young knight, well done! You will be a great horsewoman one day."

Mary Rose was so proud of herself that day. Somehow she believed every word Graham said. Once she was convinced, she would become a horse-trainer, teach humans, train horses, just like her grandfather. But since his death, she was not on track anymore. She doubted she could do it without her grandfather. She felt that people respected her because of her grandfather, but they might not engage her as a trainer alone. But maybe she needed to convince them. Surely, some of the people who engaged Graham and her only as a team would not want her on her own. But certainly, she could find students and clients who wanted her as a horse-trainer. She decided that she would take on some clients after her return. She just needed to gather her strength and gain new confidence. She could do it.

Mary Rose stood up and walked back towards the cottage. When she came back to the cottage, her parents were on the way out to the car.

"We are invited for dinner at Gordon's place tonight. Annemarie will join as well. We'll come and pick you up in an hour," her mother said and then they drove off.

Mary Rose stood in front of the cottage and watched the car driving along the winding road and disappearing between the hills.

THE SPELL

*R*osmarie had fallen under the spell of the unicorn. Since she had found out that it was her family's emblem, she was fascinated by it. She had a feeling that it was somewhere inside her. She had always been fascinated by horses. She had always felt that magical force of attraction drawing her to them, despite her mother's and her grandfather's ban on horses. She had been a good and obedient child. She usually did not ignore the wishes and orders of her parents and grandparents, but in this case it had been different. She just needed to be with horses. The desire to be with a horse eventually became so strong that she ignored her mother's rule that forbade her to ride horses.

One summer she was on holiday at her grandparents' farm, where she got to know another girl of her age. It turned out that her family had a Haflinger and a Noriker horse. They became friends. Rosmarie often asked if she could go and play with her. But when she was with her friend, she would spend every minute with the horses. She loved them. In secret, she learned to ride and to care for horses. When she got older, she started to take riding lessons at a riding school near the town where her parents lived. She told her parents that she was taking dance classes. Apart from that, she couldn't remember ever having lied to her parents. But there was a drive within her, something that just called her to ride.

She wanted to make her dream come true. Her parents had given her money for her eighteenth birthday, without knowing what it was she was planning to do with it. She was going to buy a horse. And now she found out that her family had always kept horses. The unicorn was on the family's coat of arms. Maybe she just followed an old instinct. Maybe she was born to ride. But what happened that made the family stop keeping horses? And what happened to that mysterious first fiancée of her grandfather? Why did her grandfather believe that horses were cursed? What terrible things had happened, that turned him against these wonderful creatures?

Rosmarie's life was suddenly upside down. How in the world was it possible that neither she, her mother, nor her grandmother knew what had happened? She wanted to know the truth. She had the right to know about her family's history, didn't she? How could she convince her grandfather that it was important for her to know? She was trying to find her path and her place in the world. She was trying to figure out what she wanted to do after she finished school. Maybe it could help her find her identity. Maybe the secret history of her family could shed some light on the current state of family relations? She needed to know. But how would she find out? Her grandfather had never been talkative, and now, since he was really old, he did not talk at all for days. His voice had become hoarse and shaky. He would get upset if she asked him. She worried that might not be good for his old heart.

She spent some time searching the internet, but she could not find out much about the unicorn. According to several sources it was a symbol for liberty and power and it was often used as heraldic beast on coats of arms. Well, that she already knew. It was on the flag of her hometown - a black, rearing unicorn. She had seen it on other flags as well, in various colours, but mostly it was white. But she could neither find out anything specific about the regional meaning of the unicorn nor could she find out anything about her family's coat of arms. She made plans to go to the local museum, with its library, and records about the history of the valley. Maybe there was a record on the family clans and their emblems? Maybe she could find out something about the lord who brought the horse to Friedrich? Maybe she could find out where he had the horses from? Maybe she could buy such a horse?

The thought stuck in her head. She wanted to imagine her parents' faces when she came by riding along on the back of a beautiful white horse - one that looked like the unicorn on the family's emblem! Could they forbid her to keep such a horse? Would they understand, that she was under the spell of the horses and just needed to follow her calling? Would they be upset?

Rosmarie had already been planning her purchase for a long time. She had reserved a place in a stable with a playpen and big pastures, where the horses were kept free-roaming in a herd. She had talked to the insurance company and she had already bought equipment for the horse. She had everything in place but the horse itself. She just needed to summon up the courage, because she was worried that this could open up a family argument. In the worst case, she might have to be able to keep the horse without the support of her parents or grandparents. Of course, she clung to the hope that her parents and grandparents would change their minds, once they saw how happy Rosmarie was with her horse.

She smiled, when she thought of Frieda and how she had figured out what Rosmarie was planning in secret. She was glad to know that she had her support. Wasn't she amazing? Her grandmother was always positive and kind, supportive and encouraging. How did she manage to keep her positive mood despite Viktor's grumpiness? It seemed as if she became the more affirmative and positive, the grumpier grandfather Viktor was. Rosmarie laughed out loud. Funny, wasn't it?

She was glad to know, she had at least her grandmother on her side. Her power was generally underestimated. At first sight, she seemed to be a friendly person who just wanted to please everybody, but behind the scenes, she was holding the reins. And in most cases, grandfather Viktor followed her advice, respected her wishes and obeyed if she asked him for something. Also, Rosmarie's mother Viktoria listened to her mother's advice. This made Frieda a powerful ally.

Rosmarie thought that she needed to bring her other grandmother, Maria Rosa, onto her side as well. Her other grandmother had had an almost fatal injury when she was a young woman and had never entirely recovered. She sat in a wheelchair most of the time since she could not walk alone without support. Also, she sometimes seemed to be very absent-minded. Sometimes she seemed to be confused. She had been like this as long as Rosmarie knew her. Grandfather Erhard said that she had lost her memory entirely and that it only came back to her bit by bit. He said it took years until she had recovered, more or less. But despite that, she was a wise woman and her grandfather listened to her and so did her son: Rosmarie's father Engelbert. So she might be another powerful ally.

Rosmarie knew that Maria Rosa liked horses, because there was a painting of a horse on the wall in the living room of their cabin in the mountains - at least as far as she remembered. Rosmarie tried to visualise the paintings in detail. Wasn't it a white horse in a dense green forest? Yes, indeed, now Rosmarie remembered. They had a painting of a white horse in the forest in their living room, beside the tiled stove. It had fascinated Rosmarie when she was little. Actually, now she thought about it, Rosmarie thought there were also white horses on the window shutters, which her grandmother had painted in fresh green and white. And the blanket her grandmother had knitted for her when she was a child, also had a white horse on it. Now Rosmarie wondered if her grandmother was also under the spell of horses? If so maybe she would support Rosmarie in the fulfilment of her dearest wish.

WRITTEN IN THE STARS

Mary Rose got into the car and drove with her parents and her grandmother over to uncle Gordon's place. There was an awkward silence in the car. Nobody talked. James just drove. Her uncle lived just on the other side of the hilltop, but for her grandmother it was too far to walk. Dusk was falling and the old manor looked almost mystical. It was built from grey stones and it had an old clocktower besides the main building. To the one side were the stables and the hay loft and the whole courtyard was surrounded by a wall. To the front there was a big wooden gate with a small gate tower. The gateway led over a bridge across a stream. Fog rose from the water and joined the smoke that came from the chimney and surrounded the place with a veil of mist. They drove down the winding road, over the bridge, through the open gate and entered the courtyard. Another car entered behind them, it was her brother Jonathan. Mary Rose was surprised her brother had come. She did not see him often. He was older than Mary Rose and much more similar in nature to their parents. He was about to graduate from law school, and he would become a barrister or the junior partner in her father's office. He had not been to Scotland for a long time. Mary Rose thought it was about time for him to visit their grandmother.

They got out of the car and entered the house through the giant oak door at the front entrance. Her uncle Gordon and her cousin George were expecting them and welcomed them in the entrance hall. They all shook hands and made polite conversation. They were guided through the corridor that was stuffed with antiques that belonged to the ancestors of their family. There were portraits, suits of armour for horse and rider, arms, and a flag with a unicorn on it. Gordon opened the door to the dining room. There was a long table that was already set for dinner. It was also made from oak, just as the chairs and the bookcase. They took a seat at the table and Gordon served them drinks and he looked around and said:

"Let me guess: water for Mary Rose, tea for Annemarie, beer for George, champaign for Annabelle and whiskey for James, Jonathan and myself?"

Everybody nodded. It seemed that habits had not changed since the family got together the last time. That must have been a while ago.

Mary Rose tried her very best to be a good daughter and please her parents. She had washed and brushed her hair and put on a dress and shoes rather than her usual riding boots. She really tried very hard. She wanted to make her parents happy. But it was just that they were so disturbingly different. Mary Rose had the feeling that her wishes and desires were quite the opposite of what her parents wanted. She never intended to upset her parents. She wanted them to be proud of her. But it just seemed that she put them off whenever she was trying to be herself, and whenever she followed the path that she thought was right for her.

So she was looking neat this evening and tried to behave like a lady, and she felt that her parents greatly appreciated her making the effort. Initially, the atmosphere was relaxed and pleasant, until her parents started nagging her about her travel plans again. They wanted to know where she was going and what her plans were. They offered her a place to stay for the summer at the manor of one of her father's friends who had bought a vineyard in France. They invited her to join them sailing on the Mediterranean Sea all summer long. They would love to have her on the boat, they said. Mary Rose saw the disappointment on her parents' faces when she said she did not want to come sailing. They kept nagging her, and finally her cousin George blurted out:

"She is planning to ride the horse across Europe!"

Mary Rose shot him a most reproachful look. Of course she had told uncle Gordon about her plans. George must have listened. That was typical of him.

"What?" Her parents said at the same time.

"No, we won't allow that! That is too dangerous. It is dangerous enough that you ride along the beach as if you needed to win the Great National race, but all across Europe? What are you thinking? No way!"

Mary Rose took a deep breath. "You don't need to

worry. I will ride slowly and I will take care. I will plan the journey in detail and I will have a place to stay every night. I will ride just a few miles each day - very slowly - and then I'll spend the night at a horse-stable or a farm, and then the next day I'll ride a few more miles, and so on. There is absolutely nothing to worry about."

"Why would you want to do that? Darling, we can drive you and your horse to the most beautiful places in Europe. Wherever you want to go, we can take you there. And you can go for a ride there."

"I want to travel by horse. Why are you sailing across the Mediterranean?"

Her mother looked over at Annemarie indignantly. "This is your fault! You always told her your old stories! You always encourage her to do crazy horse stuff!"

Annemarie just shrugged her shoulders.

It was silent for a moment. Then Mary Rose spoke with a quiet voice: "You know what I would really wish for? I wish the two of you would once - just one time in your life - try to understand me. If you could just once try to acknowledge the wishes of your daughter."

Her parents looked embarrassed and also a bit confused. Mary Rose understood that they really had no idea what this was all about.

"Darling, we are doing our best. And we want the best for you. We want you to be safe. Horse riding is so dangerous. It has the most fatal injuries of any sports."

"But I don't ride for sport. I am not racing, I am not show-jumping over six-foot obstacles. I just do a little bit of Horsemanship and some Liberty Training, every now and then I go for a gentle Sunday ride, and now I am

going on a trekking ride. I am not doing anything irre-
sponsible."

"Darling, I have seen you riding bareback and
without bridle and reins - and without a helmet too.
Don't tell me that is not dangerous."

"I am one of the best horse trainers in Scotland. Trust
me, I know what I am doing. But that is the point: you
don't trust me. You never did. You just cannot take my
word that I am doing the right thing. You don't believe
in me. You don't believe that I will find my way. And that
is what hurts most of all."

Mary Rose felt really sad after she said that. In fact, it
hurt her deeply and it made her feel bad at the same time
that she hurt her parents. She knew they wanted the best
for her, but they had always discouraged her doing
'horse-stuff' as they called it. Maybe that was part of the
reason why she had eventually stopped working as a
horse-trainer. Her grandfather had always encouraged
her. But now he was dead. And the discouraging side
gained more influence.

The atmosphere had collapsed and it was silent for a
moment.

Then uncle Gordon cleared his throat and
announced: "Since it is Mary Roses's birthday, I am
delighted to pronounce that we are having a meat-free
dinner tonight. Bring the vegetables on my son!"

That made Mary Rose smile. How kind was it of
uncle Gordon to consider her wish for vegetarian food
and cook vegetables for dinner! She was pleased and
thanked her uncle Gordon. George carried a huge plate
of roasted vegetables and potatoes. It smelled deliciously
of herbs and spices. He went to the kitchen again and

returned with various salads and put them on the table. It was a feast. Mary Rose's mood improved with the first bite. Eating dinner generally improved the atmosphere. Everybody seemed to be happy whilst they were eating. The food tasted delicious and everybody liked it. Afterwards, Mary Rose stepped outside to get some fresh air and look at the stars. The night was starlit and quiet. She wondered, what was written in the stars. Was she meant to become a horse-trainer, a lawyer or something else? Was it up to herself to rewrite the stars?

"Hi darling," a voice said behind her.

It was Annabelle. She came close up to Mary Rose and stopped besides her. She looked into the starlit sky as well.

"What are you doing out here? It is cold."

"I am just looking at the night-sky and wondering if I can rewrite what's written in the stars."

"I am sure you can. You can be anything you want to. Why don't you tell me what's going on?"

"Because I am scared that you won't understand and you will stop me."

"Give me a chance."

"It is grandma's last wish. I shall return the gift that was given to her. I want to do it."

Annabelle took a deep breath of cold air. Mary Rose risked a glance at her. She saw how her eyes widened and she saw that she started to grasp the whole dimension of her daughter's plan. She was overwhelmed and it took her some time to digest that.

After a while she said: "I see."

It was silent for a while.

"Actually, I think now I start to understand what this

really is about. I am still not happy that you are going to do this, but I understand. If you have to do it, then do it. But please make sure that you stay safe."

"Thanks mum. I am glad to hear that. I want to do it. I am a bit worried myself, but determined. I have to do it for grandma, but its is more than this, it is a point of honour to return the gift."

"Yes, it is." Annabelle agreed.

They stood side by side in silence for while and looked up to the sky. Then Annabelle said: "She waited for you to grow up."

"Yes, I think so too."

"I was not assertive enough to handle horses. They never respected me as their leader."

"That's because you are scared. They sense that."

"True. But I also felt it is wrong to ride them when you don't love them as much as you, mum and dad do."

"That's why you left right? Because you did not like it that animals were used on the farm?"

"Yes, and that is what we have in common: We are the first two vegetarians in the family."

"Yes, and we are converting the family. Can you believe we had a feast without meat being served? Amazing!"

"Yes, indeed, that is amazing." They smiled at each other. Then Annabelle added: "But it is also the reason why I am encouraging you to consider other options as well. You might get fed up with training horses for people who do not respect them."

Mary Rose nodded. "I promise I will consider other options."

They smiled at each other. Then Annabelle put her

arm around Mary Rose's shoulders and said: "Let's go back in. It is cold outside."

They went back inside. Gordon was playing the bagpipes and George and Jonathan were dancing. It turned into a lively family party.

THE HIGHLANDS

*T*he following morning Rosmarie got up early. She went down to the kitchen. Her grandmother gave her a cup of tea and a bowl of Riebel, a traditional farmers' dish made from millet semolina and served with apple puree. Then she went to the stable and helped her uncle Vinzent milk their fifteen cows. When they came back to the house, Frieda had prepared a second breakfast. There was homemade bread, butter and honey. Everything was from their own fields, cows and bees. Rosmarie usually followed a vegan diet when she was living in town, but when she stayed at her grandparents' farmhouse, she made an exception and ate dairy. The cows of her family were kept well and they had kept dairy cows for generations, dairy farming was her ancestors way of life. She put butter and honey on her bread.

After the mid-morning snack, Rosmarie and her uncle Vinzent got into the jeep. She opened the door and found her grandfather on the front seat, so she hopped into the back of the car. That meant that he wanted to come for the ride. Her grandfather Viktor was very old and he could not walk the stairs alone anymore, but he still wanted to come and see what was going on. Uncle Vinzent always joked that he was just a control freak and he liked to give orders whilst sitting on a bench, holding onto his stick, glaring through his monocle. He was probably right, Rosmarie thought. He liked to be in charge and tell others what to do. This was about the only time he ever talked. Vinzent got into the car and drove towards the mountains, up the winding road to the water reservoir. Further along, the road narrowed, and they followed a slanted and dangerous route next to the ravine.

"That must be where Friedrich found the lord in the ravine," Rosmarie said in a conversational tone, but as loud as possible, because her grandfather did not hear well anymore.

Viktor looked at her with a hint of surprise. But he nodded.

"Yes, probably," he replied with his hoarse voice. "The ravine is dangerous. Many people have died in there. The road is narrow and steep. Not everybody can get past it safely. Some people say the ravine is the gate to the highland valley and protects it. The ravine swallows some, but lets others pass. Sometimes the river swells from a peaceful stream to a thunderous torrent, tearing away bridges and carrying away whole trees. And further up in the highlands, the ravine is even steeper with several side arms. Those cut through the valley from both sides and they are quite tricky. There are stories of people who fell into the ravine when it was stormy and foggy and they could not see anything."

Now Rosmarie was surprised. It was a rare occasion that her grandfather spoke more than a few words. That was very unlike him. Rosmarie hoped that he would tell her something more - more stories. But that was it. She left it there. She knew her grandfather had made an effort, and did not want to place too many demands on him. The car crawled up the narrow road along the ravine. The snow chains burrowed through the snow. Then they crossed the bridge. The most dangerous part was behind them now. Rosmarie was relieved. Now the road led through the beginnings of the highlands. From this needle's eye upwards the plain of the highland valley got broader and broader, and gradually flattened out. When they drove around the last curve through the forest, the highland valley opened in front of them. Rosmarie relaxed. She sighed.

If one passed the road along the ravine and through the steep forest, then one was rewarded with a wonderful view of the beautiful mountain scenery. The plain opened up on both sides. The river was gentle and murmuring. It was hard to imagine, that this was the same river as the thunderous cascade of water that roared through the ravine further down. The landscape was covered with a thick layer of snow, which glittered in the sun. And on the horizon, at the end of the valley, on top of the world, there were the majestic towers. These giant mountains towered over the whole highland valley. They were Rosmarie's favourite mountains. And this valley - the highland valley of her ancestors - was her favourite place on Earth - well the second, right after the back of a horse. It somehow made her feel connected to the history of her family - about which she knew so little, as she just had found out.

She took renewed courage from the beautiful mountain scenery and her feelings of connection to the place, the family, the history.

'If not now, then when?' Rosmarie thought by herself.

Now was a chance to try to have a conversation with her grandfather. He was not often in the mood to talk. So she risked another attempt.

"My mum used to tell me a story of my great-great-grandmother Susanna, who almost fell into the ravine during a blizzard. But the cows stopped and so she was warned there was the gorge. And then a horse led her to a shed."

Grandfather Viktor again seemed to be surprised. But he nodded again. "Yes, this story was told in our family. It was handed down from one generation to the next."

"And Frieda says, we have a white horse on our family's coat of arms. I like horses. They are beautiful and they seem to bring luck to our family."

Grandfather Viktor froze. He did not nod. He just fell into silence. Rosmarie resisted asking him about the white horses. She did not want to push it too far. It had been a long conversation in her grandfather's terms. She gazed at him from the side, but she did not say anything.

At her grandfather's alpine cabin, the car stopped. Vinzent turned off the motor and left the car. He did not seem to care about old stories. Viktor stayed seated in the car and was staring straight ahead. Rosmarie did not move. She had the feeling that he was gathering himself, and maybe there was more to come? She was waiting patiently.

Finally, Viktor started to speak: "The horses brought great luck and high esteem to the family. But they also caused misfortune and pain. You should be aware of that too. There is a fateful side to them as well."

He left the car without another word. Rosmarie waited until her emotions settled. Her heart was racing. She had thought for a moment that he would tell her what had happened. She calmed down a little bit and she got out of the car.

Her uncle was inspecting the roof. Rosmarie helped him. She climbed up the ladder to the top of the alpine hut and shovelled the snow off the roof. Together with Vinzent she inspected the tiles and they found that they had withstood the load of snow. Then they repeated their inspection with the second roof. Her grandfather nodded at her acknowledging. That was his way of saying thank you. Rosmarie knew that. So she said: "You are welcome."

Vinzent offered to drive her up to the alpine hut with the restaurant, where she worked. But Rosmarie thanked him. She said she wanted to walk a little bit before she started work. She decided not to mention that she also did not want her uncle to drive up further, where the snow got thicker still. Anyway, she liked the hike through the highlands up to the mountain hut. The surroundings were wonderful. She sensed that every time she came here and felt a bit lost - torn between the mountain valley and the town - she felt better as soon as she started walking. When she dropped into a rhythmic walk and walked through the mountain valley, she found peace.

She said good-bye to her grandfather and her uncle, and set off. The day was beautiful. The sky was clear. Rays of sunshine rose up behind the high peaks, reflecting a golden light on the Towers. Somehow, when Rosmarie walked through the highlands, she felt grounded. She walked on the same ground as her mother did, when she was young. It was the ground on which her grandparents lived today. It was the same ground on which Friedrich had walked, as well as Susanna. It gave her a feeling of belonging. When she looked up and she saw the incredible vista of the highland valley, dotted with tiny little huts and sheds that had barely changed in two hundred years, it was almost like traveling back in time. She could imagine Friedrich and Susanna living in the same hut as her grandparents did now.

She turned around and saw her grandfather standing in front of the hut. In her mind, she added a horse to this perfect picture and smiled. Then she carried on her way.

HOME IS WHERE THE HORSE IS

*I*t was early in the morning when Mary Rose took the horses for a ride. She wanted to be back before her parents arrived for breakfast. Mary Rose had a fitful sleep last night and she needed to recharge her batteries and calm down. The best way for her to do this was to go for a ride: the best place in the world was on the back of a horse, Mary Rose thought. One of the most beautiful places in the world to go for a ride was along the coast and across the headland, which was Mary Rose's home. She was born there. Her parents had planned to be back in London when she was born. But she had come two weeks early, while her parents were on holiday in Scotland. She felt that she belonged here.

Most of all, she had always loved the horses. On the horseback, she felt safe. Whenever she felt lost, when-ever she needed to recharge, when she needed to find her roots and her strength, when she needed to be comforted and gain new courage and self-confidence, she took the horses for a ride and it made all her worries go away. People say that home is where your heart is, and for Mary Rose that was where her horses were. Belonging was especially tied to the horses and her grandmother.

As soon as she sat on the back of her horse, she experienced stress relief. Horses were present. Horses were attentive. Their presence brought her back into the here and now. And if the here and now meant sitting on a horse and riding across the headland towards the coast, how could one not feel better immediately? She was very grateful for this. She knew that she was lucky.

After a ride across the headland, towards the cliff, and down along the beach, Mary Rose felt composed again. She felt centred and balanced. She felt in harmony with her surroundings. She was present, calm, and powerful - just as her horses were. When they reached the green land on top of the cliff, she got off the horse, stroked its neck, and signalled to the horses that they were allowed to graze. Mary Rose sat down with a view on the sea, the horizon and the sky. By her side, the horses started grazing. As soon as she heard the rhythmic sound of them pulling at the grass, she sensed a feeling of deep peace. She thanked the horses for being here, for their presence and for the peace that they gave her. She meditated to the rhythmic sound of grazing horses. It was her favourite meditation.

After a while, she got up and rode back. She returned to the cottage of her grandmother with a smile on her face. Her parents, her uncle and her grandmother were sitting on the terrace in front of the cottage. Her grandmother smiled at her as she came closer. She liked to see her granddaughter riding. She enjoyed watching the harmony between horses and people. Her father looked skeptically. He still thought of horses as wild and unpredictable animals that could be dangerous when startled. That was true of course, but not if one built a solid relationship of trust and respect. And this was Mary Rose's speciality: training a horse on the basis of trust and respect and forming a relationship that was stronger than their fear and their reflex for flight. There was a reason why she was renowned in the horse community for her Liberty Training with horses. She was not just a teenager doing reckless things with a horse but was very responsible in her practice. She was an expert and she knew what she was doing.

She stopped the horses near the cottage terrace, got off and thanked them. She stroked their foreheads and whispered words of gratitude in their ears. Then she sent them off to graze. She stepped onto the terrace with a smile.

"What a wonderful morning it is! And how wonderful is it to go for a morning ride. I feel truly happy."

Her grandmother and her uncle nodded approvingly. Also her mother nodded hesitantly.

"Every time I go for a ride, I feel fully recharged afterwards. It is a magic remedy. Whenever I feel down or anxious, if I go for a ride, I feel better instantly."

Grandmother Annemarie smiled. "Yes, that is the effect of horses. I know exactly what you mean. I always felt safe as soon as a horse was with me."

"Yes, they radiate a sense of safety and belonging.

Once you gain their trust, and they accept you, the herd feels just like family," Gordon added.

James looked skeptically. He might have never had a thought like this before.

"Yes, that is true. It is wonderful to be part of the herd," Mary Rose agreed. She smiled at her uncle.

Mary Rose went inside to get breakfast. When she came back from the kitchen with a tray of food and plates, she heard her grandmother saying:

"You feel at home where your heart is bound to."

Mary Rose had not heard the beginning of the conversation, but she guessed and she added: "Yes, and that means my home is where the horses are." She laughed.

She put the tray down and went back into the kitchen to get the rest of the breakfast. When she returned to the terrace James glanced at her with a cheeky grin.

"Alright, if home is where the horse is, then we just need to kidnap the horse and take it to Oxford."

"Dad! No, they cannot be kept in a stable. They are free-roaming horses."

"Well, then you might have to go back and forth. And you could come visit us in London more often too. Maybe it is not one way or the other, maybe you can have both."

"I will think about studying on the ride. I promise."

"And since I was now informed about the true background of this long-distance ride, I am pleased to tell you one thing you did not know about your father: He once did a bicycle ride all the way from Scotland to France. And we will call everybody on the way and ask them to give you shelter for the night and make sure you'll be safe." Annabelle smiled at her daughter.

"Here, this is for you," James said and handed Mary Rose an old compass and a modern satnav.

"It is from my father. He was a sailor. He was convinced the compass brings luck. He never got lost."

"Thank you!"

Mary Rose gave her parent a hug. She was glad. The world had changed overnight.

THE VALLEY OF THE ANCESTORS

*R*osmarie fell into a rhythmic walk. Walking was like meditation to her. After a few minutes, she could feel her mind stop its incessant buzzing, and put to rest all the nagging questions. Then the walking started to work its wonders and she realised how she could be there in the moment without even thinking at all. She just walked and took in the mountain scenery, the forest and the path in front of her. Through walking everything became one again. At least, she became one again. She was herself, walking her path, without asking herself all these questions about her future and her past. She knew the questions would come back, but as long as she kept walking, she could forget about them.

She wandered along the torrent and climbed the path amongst the big rocks. Trees grew between the boulders, and rays of sunlight shone through the tree tops. Snow covered the forest floor. Everything was white, glittering, and sparkling, in an almost fairy tale landscape. Somehow she could imagine that it would be the perfect habitat for a unicorn. She could almost sense its spirit. A breeze blew powder snow from a branch and the wind carried the crystals through the air. The snow crystals glistened in the sun and filled the air with glittering fairy dust. Rosmarie opened her arms towards the sky and laughed. She let the snow crystals land on her face and she giggled with joy. She felt like a fairy in a magical land.

'Oh, how beautiful this place is,' she thought. 'I understand why my family clan settled here. It is truly amazing. It is no surprise that people tell stories about unicorns up here. It looks like a unicorn forest. Everything is white and glittering between tall trees and high mountains.'

She followed the road through the forest along the gently bubbling brook. Icicles were on both sides of the torrent, on everything that touched the water. When Rosmarie came out of the forest onto the wide open plain of the pastures, she saw a long icicle that grew from the roof of a hay shed. She picked it and looked at it.

'That looks like a unicorn horn,' she thought.

She laughed about her blooming phantasy. Yes, she was caught by the spell of the unicorn. She suddenly saw unicorns everywhere. She held it into the sunlight. It looked truly magical in the light. It was shiny and transparent. Its surface was perfectly smooth, and it looked like it was made of crystal glass. She felt like a super heroine when she held the unicorn horn into the sunlight.

"I am a knight of the unicorn! Give me the power! I will do everything I can for them. I will always be kind, honest and brave. Dear unicorns, accept me as a follower of your clan. I am a descent of Friedrich - the first knight of the unicorn in this valley."

In her imagination she saw a sparkling light at the edge of the forest. Then a shiny white silhouette came closer. It was a unicorn! It stood still in front of her, until she kneeled down. When she bowed her head, it knighted her. She felt the light flowing through her body and a feeling of incredible, inexhaustible power. When she got up, she felt a new strength. She felt a calling, as if she had been chosen to watch over the valley. She felt as if she had been awarded a scroll with special rights, and a magical force that supplied her with the strength, the vigour and the power of a horse. She felt, that she carried the power of a horse within her. It made her feel invincible. It made her feel powerful. She felt, that whatever was to come, she would be able to handle it.

She continued walking through the glittering winter forest on the other side of the plain. Every now and then she saw a light, a sparkle, shining brightly in the snow between the trees, and she imagined that the light came from the unicorn. Just as it had been told in the book of sagas. Then, she thought about her ancestress, who had to flee to the mountains and lived in the woods, because a woman had died in childbirth. How did she survive the winter up here, Rosmarie wondered. She must have collected herbs, berries, mushrooms and roots all summer long. And maybe, she fished in the lake. Did she hunt?

'No,' Rosmarie shook her head.

She wanted her ancestress to be a peaceful woman who could not bring herself to kill an animal. She imagined how she would have strolled through the forests with the white horse by her side. The rabbits and the birds would greet her without fear. She would collect plants and prepare meals from what she foraged. In summer she would go foraging every day, so she had enough for winter. And she had a little vegetable garden in front of her hut. She would have planted grains and made hay, to feed the animals in the winter.

Rosmarie stopped. The wind carried snow crystals through the air and for a second they formed the shapes of a white horse and a woman. It was a vision. She tried to sense their spirit. Somehow it made her feel connected to the place, but also to the past, and to her family when she thought about her ancestress who walked with the unicorn.

'Strange,' Rosmarie thought, 'how is this possible? I've never felt rooted and I've never felt really connected to my family. Throughout my childhood and youth they were always arguing, blaming one another and not keeping together. But suddenly, it's all changed. I hear a few old stories, and I have visions about my ancestress, the witch I never met, and about my ancestor Friedrich. Suddenly, I feel like I come from a family of witches and knights who always kept horses. I always dreamt of horses without knowing my family history, without knowing that my family always kept horses, without knowing the family had a coat of arms. Maybe, the horse is the key? Maybe, if I get a horse, I will find myself, I will understand, who I really am. And maybe then, I will be able to reconcile my family. Maybe, it is the horse that is missing? Maybe the horse is the missing piece of the puzzle? Maybe one day everything will fall in place?'

Rosmarie took off her coat and put it on a tree trunk in the sunshine, next to the torrent that burbled along the forest. She sat down and she talked quietly into the forest. In her thought she spoke to her ancestress:

"Dear ancestress, whom I never met. Do you want to be my patroness? I think I need a patroness. I choose you. I want you because you are the woman who walked with the unicorns. I admire you. I often doubt that I am good enough, strong enough, and that I will be able to handle a horse by myself without help. Can you support me? I want a horse, but I want to treat it right. I am not convinced of the methods they are teaching me in the sports stable. I want to do things differently. I want to become a horse whisperer. I want to learn Horsemanship. Do you think I will manage to learn that by myself?" For a moment she imagined herself training before she added: "I will try, for sure."

Rosmarie sighed. She felt better for having chosen her patroness - the ancestress who had spent her life up her in the mountain forests.

KNIGHTHOOD

*O*n her morning ride, Mary Rose rode past the manor of her ancestors. Today, her uncle was working outside at the gate and the bridge. He looked up when he saw the horse coming towards him.

"My favourite niece, nice of you to come visit your uncle before you head off. Can I offer you a cup of tea?"

Mary Rose agreed. They went inside and Mary Rose sat down at the kitchen table. Uncle Gordon put the kettle on the stove. The kitchen of the manor was still very much like it has always been. A stove and firewood were used to cook. The table was hand-carved and made from oak wood. Then uncle Gordon took a seat as well and asked her:

"Is there something on your mind, my dear? You know that you can talk about anything with me. Please share your thoughts and your worries with your uncle, and allow him to give you some of his wisdom if he can."

Mary Rose sighed. She thought about it for a while.

She was not able to fully grasp all of her worries, which made it even more difficult to find words for them.

"I worry about grandma. I know you will look after her. But she asked me to fulfill her 'last' wish. I want to do this for her, of course. But I also worry that I might be far away and not be able to say goodbye when she leaves this Earth. On top of that, I worry that I might be too weak and unable to complete the journey, or that I will experience difficulties on the way, or that I might not find the person, or that she is dead, or that something will happen to the horse that is beyond my control. And I feel that I disappoint my parents and I am unable to live up to their expectations. I'm struggling to balance my own desires with the wishes of my parents."

Gordon nodded and stroked his beard.

"I understand. I already suspected some of this. For the reasons you have already mentioned, I think this journey will be important for you. Your grandmother will not live forever. There are things that are outside your control. Those things, you will not be able to change. But regarding your journey, you can be as prepared as possible, and you can do everything you can, to succeed in spite of the challenges ahead. You are a descendant of knights, and I am sure you will do everything you can to fulfil your grandmother's last wish. But if you want to be on the safe side, we can use the time before your departure to work on your knightly skills. Maybe that will help you gain confidence in your abilities. Knighthood is something one needs to work for. It requires training, practice and knowledge to develop the right skills. A lot of it you have learned since your early childhood. A lot of the training, your great-grandfather Gareth and your grandfather Graham have taught you. But I can help you refresh your skills."

Mary Rose nodded gratefully. "Yes, that would be good. I want to train hard and be in the best possible shape, when I set out on this journey."

"Come!"

Gordon got up and walked out of the kitchen along the corridor and entered the library. It was a room with high ceiling and bookshelves that reached almost up to it. To the other side were big windows and the morning sun put the library into a golden light. It smelled of a lot of really old books. Gordon climbed up to the higher level of the bookshelf and took some books with him. He put them on the table and said to Mary Rose:

"I suggest that you read all of these books, and that you come here every day to practice survival skills and martial arts. Can you come in the mornings?"

"Yes, Sir! I will come every morning, as soon as I have taken care of the horses and grandma."

"Excellent! But let's not waste time. Let's start your first lesson today. For today's homework, I would encourage you to choose two of the books, read at least the first chapter of each, and tell me tomorrow what you have learned."

Mary Rose nodded. She picked a book with the title 'The Secret Skills of the Knights' and one which was called 'Living off the Wild - Foraging Wild Plants in Europe'.

"Good choices!" Gordon's nod was approving. "Oh, and here, I have a gift for you," he said.

He opened the chest of the old desk and handed her a

book called 'The Amazon Warriors and other mounted female knights in ancient myths'.

Mary Rose smiled. He had been expecting her. He had already prepared a present for her.

"Thank you. You were waiting for me to come," she said.

"Oh well, I was prepared. This is such an important chapter in your life. Of course I have thought about a present."

Mary Rose was touched. Her uncle seemed to understand her and know what was going on with her without her having to say a word.

"Alright, I am ready for my lesson."

Gordon lead her to the courtyard, where the horse was waiting and suggested: "You relax and take a nap. Take the saddle off, put it on the ground and nap. When I ring the bell, I want you to take all you belongings, saddle your horse and disappear, before I get back down here. Be fast, efficient, silent and invisible." He pointed to the bell of the old clock tower. "I am going up there now."

Mary Rose leaned against the saddle and tried to relax. 'Actually,' she thought, 'that is a good exercise. Why had it never occurred to me?'

She was able to handle her horse perfectly, but always under perfect conditions. What if she had to hurry? What if the horse felt that she was stressed and nervous? What if the horse did not obey when she was anxious? Actually, she had to admit that this horse would need some special training to cope with stressful situations. This horse was the youngest, the most sensitive and the least confident of all her horses. Mary Rose herself was no longer sure if she could rely on her horse when she herself was stressed. But she would find out.

In that moment, the bell rang. The horse lifted its head and its ears twitched quickly. Obviously it did not like the sound. Mary Rose had probably got up too rapidly. The horse snorted suspiciously. Mary Rose tried to move quickly but calmly, so as not to disturb the horse further. But she knew she was losing time. The horse had stepped away, and she had to follow it with the saddle. It also did not lower its head straight away as it usually did, but held it up, listening to the bell. More precious seconds slipped away. When eventually the horse was saddled and bridled, she walked with the horse towards the gate. She got in the saddle and prepared to ride off, when suddenly the gate closed. With a thunderous noise the massive wooden door slammed to the lock. The horse spooked and jumped to the side. The horse was seriously upset now.

Mary Rose tried to stay calm and think. She was locked in. There was no way out. Her horse could not jump over the wall and the fences, it was not a show-jumper. She turned the horse and looked around. She knew she did not have any more time left. Quickly, she rode towards the big wooden door, where the stables were. She opened the door, leaning over the back of the horse, and rode into the stable. The stable was empty because her uncle's horses were outside grazing in the fields. She led the horse to the boxes. Then she climbed through the hay hatch up to the hay loft. From there, she sneaked across to the other end of the hay loft. She stopped and listened. She could hear uncle Gordon's footsteps in the courtyard. The clock tower was next to the hay loft. Mary Rose ran to the clock tower, entered and ran up the stairs to the place where she knew her great-grandfather had always kept a key for the big entrance gate. She had known about this as a child when she used to play here with her cousin, but she had not been up here for a long time. She hoped that the key would be still in the same place. She looked for it, found it, ran downstairs, opened the big gate and ran towards the stable. She pulled the door open, whistled and the horse came to her. She clambered onto its back, turned around and rode off in a gallop towards the gate.

Next to the gate, uncle Gordon was leaning with his rifle in the hand. Mary Rose stopped the horse. She had lost the game.

"You two are a perfect team when everything is nice and easy. But under stress, you both lose confidence. You must learn to stay confident in any situation. You need to trust in yourself, your abilities and also in your partner - the horse."

Mary Rose nodded. She knew uncle Gordon had a point there.

"We are used to being stress-free and relaxed."

Uncle Gordon responded by firing a shot in the air. The horse jumped with a huge leap to the side, but Mary Rose stayed in the saddle.

"You should prepare for other situations too - just in case."

Mary Rose nodded.

"I will see you tomorrow morning."

SILENCE

*R*osmarie finally took the last bend in the road. When she came around the curve, the steep rock walls to one side opened a little bit. On the other side, the thick forest thinned out, and the climb became less steep. It allowed a view of the high plateau, the highest of the valley, and the highest pasture - just underneath the scree slope at the feet of the Towers. The Towers were the highest peaks in the area, stretching high up into the sky. The road wound through the forest. The trees were smaller up here. A few hundred meters up the tree line marked the sudden end of the forest. Beyond, the boulders became bigger, the rock walls steeper, the snow and the scree thicker. The winding road led around a boulder with a clump of trees on its top. From here, she could see the alpine hut. It was a beautiful picture: The winding road, trees to either side of the road, the hut, and behind it all, the rock walls of the Towers.

Rosmarie sighed. It was a nice place up here. The alpine hut had a restaurant, a dormitory and several rooms. She went inside and said hello to the landlord and the cook. She went upstairs to her room, got changed, and came back down to start work. There were already guests. The alpine hut was a popular destination for hikers and people who went on ski hikes. A lot of pensioners and tourists came up here for day hikes. The Towers were the most impressive mountains in the Alps, at least according to Rosmarie. The highland valley was beautiful. The hut was cosy, comfortable and served good food. There were many reasons to come up here. Rosmarie had come here every holiday since she was a child. When she was younger, she had stayed with her grandparents, since she turned sixteen, she worked as a waitress in the restaurant during her holidays. Rosmarie put on her Dirndl - a traditional dress of the region. Then she went down to the kitchen and started to prepare breakfast.

A group of pensioners, all of them elderly men, came in. They had come to the alpine hut before. Rosmarie recognised their faces. Most of them were at least seventy. Two of them seemed to be older than the others. Rosmarie was impressed that they had managed to get up here despite their age. It was easily two and a half hours' march from the bus-stop at the water reservoir. However, both of them had a german shepherd, and Rosmarie suspected that the dogs had pulled their old masters up to the mountain hut. The group sat down at a long table next to the fire place. They were all hungry and thirsty and asked for beer, even though it was early in the morning. Rosmarie was astounded about how much these old people ate and drank. Her own grandparents drank hardly any alcohol and they ate much less than Rosmarie. She carried plates of soup and dumplings to their table, and meat dishes followed. She carried quite a few glasses of beer and at the end of the main course they started drinking schnapps.

After she had served all the food and drinks, Rosmarie leaned next to the kitchen door and had some of the soup herself for lunch. The cook had gone to get more wood from the stack outside for the oven. She heard how the voices of the guests grew louder, the more they drank. At one point their conversation turned to the smuggling route from here across the Tower Gate - a pass in between the high peaks on either side that was the border to Switzerland. One of the men talked over most of the others, telling all sorts of stories of smugglers, hunters and farmers who used to live up here, which he claimed were all true.

"My great-grandfather knew this mountain range inside out. He could find the way to Switzerland across the pass even in the dark. He smuggled schnapps and tobacco and sugar. It was a flourishing business. And he was never caught."

"That's only because he bribed the hunter and the policemen," one of the other men threw in.

The men laughed out loud, joked and drank more beer. Then they discussed what they were going to do with the rest of morning. Four of the men wanted to go up towards the Tower Gate now. Rosmarie thought this was a bad idea after they'd had so much alcohol. But it did not seem to worry them. The four of them went upstairs, put their stuff in the room, and left before lunch. Two went upstairs to take a nap. The rest of them just stayed at the table next to the fireplace drank beer, played cards and continued their boisterous conversation.

During lunchtime, a few other people arrived: hikers, skiers, tourists, pensioners. All of them ate and drank something, and left afterwards. Only the group of pensioners stayed. Rosmarie was starting to get worried about their alcohol levels. She told the landlord that they had had several beers and some schnapps. He said, she should tell them that the schnapps was out and she was really sorry, but the landlord could offer them a bottle of liquor instead. He pointed at the bottles of alcohol free liquor that he bought and re-labelled especially for these occasions. Rosmarie nodded. Just a few minutes later they ordered another round of schnapps and she brought them alcohol-free liquor instead. After lunch, some of the men went for a short walk, some took a nap.

Rosmarie had a break. She went for a walk outside to get some fresh air. She carried on along the path that led through the thickening forest, away from the highland pastures. She quickly sank deep into her thoughts again. She knew that she might not get any stories or answers out of her old grandfather Viktor, but she would keep nagging her grandmother, her mother, her father and her other grandfather Erhard, to tell her more about the past and what had happened.

She planned to do some research on the history of the valley. The secret tunnel of her grandparents' house came back to her mind. The witches that were burned, as well as the war, were topics that prompted silence amongst all inhabitants. It was almost impossible to find anybody who was willing to say one word about those topics. Nobody talked about it. The war had been so traumatic for the population, and had left deep traces on the consciousness of the people. And they seemed to just want to forget about it and move on. Hence, they never let slip a word about it.

"Let the past be the past," Rosmarie said quietly. That was, what her grandfather used to tell her, whenever she asked a question.

She walked for half an hour, mulling these things over, before she returned to the hut. She wanted to take a quick nap before her evening shift started. When she came back to the alpine hut, one of the old men was sitting on the bench in front of the house. His german shepherd was digging holes in the snow. He nodded when she came closer, and asked with a croaking voice:

"Young lady, where do you belong?"

Rosmarie answered in thought: 'That's exactly the question I am asking myself all the time at the moment.' However, she knew what the old man wanted to know. He was asking for her family name and where she was from, so she told him. He nodded, and he seemed to know both grandfathers, Viktor and Erhard.

"They don't like each other, I have heard," he said.

"No, they don't."

"I am sorry to hear that."

Rosmarie nodded sadly. "I think it was the war. The war destroyed my family. Something happened back then. Nobody talks about it, but the gaps remain."

The old man looked at her with interest for a while. Then he replied:

"Quite possibly. The war destroyed a lot of families.

It left deep divisions in society, and scars in peoples' minds that might never heal. I am sorry for you, young lady, but at least they are all alive."

Rosmarie nodded. "Yes, that is true. I am grateful for that. I wish I could find out more, about what happened, then maybe I could do something to change things for the better. But nobody talks to me about it."

"You are not responsible for what your grandfathers do. You might have to accept it for what it is. The war has left deep scars in some people, and rifts in families. It might not be possible to repair them."

Rosmarie nodded. "I know."

They sat in silence for a while and then he looked at her and said:

"Maybe it is your task to build a bridge. Your grand-fathers are old men now. Men become more soft-hearted with age. They might see the path they have not seen before when you shine your light on it."

Rosmarie was speechless. She did not know what to reply, so she just nodded.

Then the door swung open. The cook came out, gave Rosmarie a strict look and went to the backside of the house where the wood stack was.

"Thank you," Rosmarie whispered to the old man.

She took a deep breath before she went inside and started to take the guests' orders.

AMAZON WARRIOR

*T*he following morning Mary Rose woke before sunrise. She went to look after her grandmother, and afterwards she took care of the horses. She arrived in the early morning hours at uncle Gordon's manor. The grass was wet from the morning dew. She saw the sun rising at the horizon when she entered the gateway. Gordon was expecting her. He had prepared tea and toast. Mary Rose sipped her tea and told her uncle what she had learned.

"The book with the edible plants was very interesting. Much of this I have learnt already from grandma. She taught me about all the plants in her garden and in the countryside. We used to take long walks across the plains and hills and collect berries, herbs and mushrooms. Then she showed me how to prepare meals from what we foraged. I enjoyed reading 'The skills of the knight'. I realised that you were right - great-grandfather Gareth has taught me a lot of this - how to use a bow and arrow, a sword, riding with a lance and also being strong, keeping the mind focused and staying calm, even if I am scared or in danger. And grandfather Graham taught me the equestrian skills and how to read the horses' body language and communicate with them. It feels good to know that I grew up practicing all those skills. You were right, it does raise my self-confidence. But most of all, I enjoyed the book about the Amazon warriors. It makes me feel strong and brave when I imagine I could be like them - a woman and a warrior. Even though I believe my mission is a peaceful one, a journey to pay respect and gratitude, there might be other forces in my way that might try to hinder me. So it is good to have this in mind as well."

Gordon nodded. "Yes, indeed, Gareth has always said you were the first girl to whom he has taught the skills of the knights, but you were one of his best students - besides me of course." He grinned.

Mary Rose smiled. "Of course."

Gordon's voice took on a more serious tone: "What I am trying to tell you is that you have every reason to be confident."

Mary Rose let that settle for a moment. Finally she said: "Thank you."

"You need to believe in yourself. You are strong. You are brave. You are smart. You have all that it takes. Trust yourself."

Mary Rose nodded. "Thank you. I will try to really believe in myself. I can become a knight. I can be an Amazon warrior."

"You are a knight. Being a knight means having learnt all the skills of knighthood and mastering them.

Being a knight means acting wise, honest and brave. Being a knight is something you are, or you are not. It is you, your personality, your way of life. It is not dependent on a war or an emergency situation, where you can prove that you are heroic. What counts is that you know that you are a heroine. You don't need to prove it to anyone. Be thankful, that you don't have to endure what your grandmother had to. Be a knight of love, of light and of happiness. But if there is no other way than fighting to defend it, then fight."

Mary Rose nodded slowly. "You are right, Gordon. Thank you for reminding me. It is about me knowing who I am, not about other people knowing this."

"Exactly, you have to go your way. And if your parents do not understand that, it is something they need to learn for themselves. You have to find your path, be brave enough to walk it, strong enough to not give up. And maybe you will find even more on this journey."

"What if I am scared?"

"Fear is natural. It is a feeling that is there to warn you to be aware, to make you alert, to tell you not to be reckless. Everybody has fear, and that is good. Nobody is truly fearless. It is the way you handle fear that makes the difference. When you feel anxious, notice it, be aware, be alert and act carefully, wisely and thoughtfully. It is natural that you are scared. Honestly, it would worry me if you weren't. But you are proving you are brave because you will go on your journey in spite of your fears. You have planned everything in detail. You are preparing yourself and your partner in the best possible way. You are not riding without a goal or a plan. You are not driving an untrained horse across Europe.

You are fit, smart and you have a plan that is detailed enough, so the chances of achieving your goal are good. That is what makes the difference."

"Thank you, Gordon."

"If you want to be a knight, you have to be one in your heart."

"I am. I can feel it."

"Great! Well, then, keep this in mind. Be confident and strong. Never be arrogant or supercilious. Know who you are, and do not make yourself any smaller than you are. Be proud of who you are. Be grateful for what you are and what you have been given. Recognise your gifts and talent. Don't lose yourself in pity, don't feel sorry for yourself, don't be insecure - recognise your fears and challenge them, work through them and handle them. Be aware of your weaknesses and turn them into strengths." Gordon paused and waited for Mary Rose to nod in acknowledgement.

"If you want to spread hope, love and trust wherever you go, then you need to trust yourself first. How can you sow trust, if you do not trust yourself? How can you love, if you do not love yourself? How can you spread hope, if you yourself are shaken by doubt? I have always known you as a confident young woman. But since your grandfather died, doubt is gnawing at you."

Mary Rose nodded. "I know. You are right."

"Whatever happens, you should remember that your grandmother always told you to stay positive towards life."

Mary Rose was touched. But at the same time she felt exposed. Uncle Gordon was right, she was lost in self-pity for a while. But now it was time to get on with life.

"The horse that you will take on this journey is like you. It is the most beautiful, and possibly the strongest of all your grandmother's horses. But it is the least confident. It needs you to be confident, in order for it to be confident itself."

Mary Rose nodded almost invisibly. "I know."

"So here is your exercise: In our training sessions, I want you to refer to this horse only as unicorn, and to yourself only as knight or Amazon warrior."

Mary Rose looked at him with surprise.

"And I am the king, by the way," he said, breaking into a mischievous grin.

Mary Rose laughed. "Alright, King Gordon!"

"Excellent! So let's start your next training session, knight of the unicorn!"

THE GREAT HART

The next morning, Rosmarie got up before sunrise. She wanted to go for a quick walk, before her day started and she had to serve food all day long. She dressed quickly and went outside. The air was ice cold and fresh. She took a deep breath and puffed steam clouds out in the cold air. Everything was quiet. She loved the stillness of the mornings up here. Down in the town, where her parents lived, it was never this quiet. There was no sound. Absolute stillness filled the cold morning air. It had snowed a little bit during the night and the world was covered with a white, glittering sheet of crystals, sparkling like a fairy tale landscape. Rosmarie started walking. She took a small path through the forest where nobody usually walked. After a little while, she saw footprints where a deer had crossed the road and disappeared in the snow between the trees. Feeling spontaneous, she followed the tracks into the forest.

The trees stood closer together here and the hill became very steep. Before long, she had to scramble on all fours to climb any higher. The ascent was long, and she was exhausted by the time she reached the top. She blew big steam clouds into the air as she looked around. The track had led her straight up through the steepest and densest forest, and now she stood right in front of the vertical rock wall at the edge of the canyon. Just underneath the rock wall, the ground was surprisingly flat. Underneath these overhanging boulders the ground was dry and free of snow. It was like a natural roof. It was dry here, and sheltered from the wind. She walked along the rock wall and found a lot of deer droppings. Evidently, the deer knew this was a comfortable spot. From up here she had an amazing view over the entire highland valley.

When she reached the end of the rock wall she came across a tree formation that looked almost mystical. Several thick fir trees stood in a tight circle. The branches were thick and formed a wall that looked impenetrable from the outside. Only when one looked down from a higher point one could see it was a circle. She would not have noticed it if there had not been tracks that led through the snow directly to this circle of trees. Rosmarie was curious. She did not want to disturb the deer but somehow she felt drawn to it. She crept closer, and tried to move quietly. A strong wind blew from the opposite direction. When she reached the tree wall, she dropped to her knees and dug a tunnel in the snow so she could crawl underneath the low hanging, prickly branches. Soon she caught a glimpse of the clearing in the middle of the trees. She was astounded.

A deer stood in the middle of the clearing, eating hay that lay on top of the snow. Two rabbits were hopping around, and she saw several squirrels and birds. Rosmarie was surprised, she had spent all her holidays up here but she had never seen a deer or a rabbit before. The animals were very shy. Usually they did not allow humans to get this close to them. Rosmarie lay in the snow and watched the animals with awe. Then she crawled back slowly, quietly and carefully. She retraced her own tracks so as not to create more. She tore a branch from a fir tree and wiped out the tracks behind her. She hoped that nobody else would see the tracks. She looked up to the rock walls and she stopped in the middle of her step and froze. The rock wall rose up, hundreds of meter into the sky. At the bottom of the rock wall, there was a big stag with huge antlers. Was it real? She rubbed her eyes. She looked again. She did not trust her eyes.

A big red stag stood right at the bottom of the rock walls. It looked at her. Rosmarie froze in awe. It was a majestic animal with the biggest antlers she had ever seen. His antlers were so big, it almost looked like he was carrying a tree. His fur was red, orange, of a fiery colour. She could hardly believe what she was seeing. Was this the Great Hart - the lord of the forest? Why was it showing itself to her? It must have heard her coming. Why did it not hide? Did it want her to see it? The apparition was so overwhelming for Rosmarie and its appearance so impressive that she bowed humbly to the lord of the forest. When she looked up again, the great hart had disappeared.

Rosmarie smiled. That was a proper vision - the great

hart appeared, looked at her, and disappeared when she bowed. Rosmarie was puzzled. Was she dreaming? It was really early in the morning, and she had not been sleeping well recently. Could this all be real? Her mother had always said that she had quite a lively phantasy. And even today when she was grown up, she still liked to dream and allow her phantasy to take her on a journey to magic lands. But this deer, it had been really there.

Rosmarie shook her head and then her whole body. Then she started walking back. She carefully wiped out her tracks behind her. When she reached the path, she pulled at a branch of a fir tree that grew to the side of the path, and the snow fell off the branches and spread on the ground. It covered the tracks nicely, leaving barely a trace. Rosmarie was satisfied with the result and walked back towards the alpine hut. She continued on the path. A few meters further up she noticed that to the one side of the path the snow was not pristine anymore. It looked as if somebody else had swiped over their tracks in the snow as well.

'I wonder who that was?' Rosmarie thought. 'Who comes up here so early in the morning to feed the deer and the animals of the forest?'

It was six o'clock in the morning. Who would make their way up here so early and carry hay? This feeding lot was not one of the hunter's feeding lots. They were placed on the other side of the valley, in the light forest by the highland pastures. She followed the tracks that led along the downward path to the valley. When the tracks reached the road, they disappeared into the tracks of the snow mobile, on which the landlord brought up fresh food in the early morning. Rosmarie wanted to follow the tracks and find out, who this was, but she knew the chances were quite small. Besides, given that the tracks of the snow mobile were freshly cut and from this morning, that meant that it was time for her to start work. She walked back up to the hut and entered.

The whole day, she wondered about what she had seen this morning. Wasn't there a story about a great hart that her grandmother used to tell her when she was a child? Who was the person who fed the animals? The tree circle seemed almost manmade. It was so symmetrical. Was it the work of nature? Would this person come again? She really wanted to know who it was. She could go there and wait and see, and maybe she would find out. Was it dangerous to waylay that person? People who had secrets usually wanted to keep them secret. But she was too curious not to try. That she knew already.

"Rosmarie!"

A voice called her back into the here and now. She had drifted off into a daydream, and the cook was looking at her impatiently.

"Wake up!"

Rosmarie grabbed the tray and went to the dining room to serve tea. In the afternoon, she took a nap. She wanted to sleep in advance so she could get up early tomorrow morning. She needed to know what was going on there. So over the next few days, she got up at five and made her way down to the path from where the tracks started. She sneaked out of the house and waited in the icy cold of the morning. It was freezing. The hours were long. Nobody came. Each morning, she made her way back, disappointed. Rosmarie began to wonder if she had simply dreamt everything she had seen that morning. She was tempted to go up there and search for the tree circle. But she did not want to make new traces in the snow and risk revealing the hide. So she went back.

'That is it!' Rosmarie thought, after an unsuccessful morning vigil. 'That might be the reason why the person does not come: there is no fresh snow. In the frozen snow one would see the tracks and it would not be possible to wipe them away. Maybe I have to wait for a fresh snowfall.'

Rosmarie had to wait for three more days. They seemed to drag while Rosmarie almost burst with curiosity. Then, finally, that night it snowed again. Rosmarie got up at five and sneaked out into the cold and dark morning. It was cold, foggy and it was still snowing. She walked as quickly and quietly through the forest as she could. She hid behind a boulder with a tree on its top and waited in the cold, icy dark.

'Why am I doing this? Am I going crazy? I should go back and get some sleep and some hot tea,' she thought whilst she was shivering in the cold.

The more Rosmarie thought about her situation, the closer she came to turning back. She was cold, tired and hungry. It was dark, cold and foggy. Maybe she really was going crazy. Nobody would go out in the dark, cold, foggy night deliberately. Nobody would come. She needed to stop making up fairy tales and mythic adventures. She needed to focus on real life. Maybe she was just imagining this to escape reality? Because she was bored at school, bored at work and annoyed with her family, she just escaped into this magical and adventurous world of unicorns and witches. Who wouldn't prefer to live in the unicorn forest?

Just as her patience was running out, she saw the great hart at the bottom of the rock wall. It was such an impressive red deer with such majestic antlers, Rosmarie wondered how old he must be. A short while later, Rosmarie heard steps moving quietly through the snow. A shadowy figure came along the path, wrapped in a long coat with a hood. It climbed a boulder next to the road, and balanced along a fallen tree trunk that bridged the gap down from the boulder to the ground on the other side of the rock. Then it walked off, across the thick forest.

'Ah, that's clever, this way there are no tracks that tell that somebody left the path here. Very smart,' Rosmarie thought.

Rosmarie left the path in a similar way. She climbed a rock and a tree on top of the rock and jumped from a low hanging branch into the deep snow on the other side of the boulder. She crept towards the tree circle. Then she lay in the snow and watched the person taking off a rucksack and crawling underneath the trees. A few minutes later, the person returned wiping out the tracks in the snow. Rosmarie followed. She carefully wiped her tracks away and followed the person at a safe distance. The person walked fast and with great composure. It was not easy to keep up whilst being silent and trying to remain hidden. Rosmarie struggled to keep pace. When she came around a curve, she was startled to see a wolf in the snow. This was something she had not seen before. The mysterious figure walked right up to the wolf and they walked along the path together. Rosmarie was astonished.

But then, suddenly, she had another thought:

'Is that a wolf or is it… It looks like… - No, that is not possible.'

Rosmarie was inattentive for a second and she stumbled. The wolf turned around quickly and saw her trying to hide behind a tree. It barked once. Then it sniffed the air. Then it came towards her. There was no point trying to hide now. Rosmarie stepped out of her hiding place.

THE LAST UNICORN

*G*ordon took a sip of his tea and put the cup down. Then he spoke with his most majestic voice: "Let's get your mind focused on your skills again, and lets start a training session. I might have to make a more serious plan to test your abilities. Now, this is the Earth's last unicorn and you are the world's last knight of the unicorn. It is your purpose to defend the unicorn and guarantee its survival. I am a greedy old king who wants to drink the blood of the unicorn because he has heard that it makes humans immortal. Your task is to save the unicorn and yourself because the chances of survival are not good without you. The unicorn needs its knight."

Mary Rose felt nervous instantly, but she nodded. This was a big task. Most of all it scared her that he threatened to kill her horse. It put her under pressure. But she knew that was what Gordon wanted. Gordon was a very talented story-teller and he used the stories very effectively to teach her the lessons she needed to learn.

"You get Gareth's dagger, but don't use it, unless there is really no other way."

Mary Rose felt honoured. "Really? I get great-grand-father's dagger?"

"Of course. You are a knight of our family, and you are about to go on an important mission. You shall carry the dagger of your ancestors. It will keep you safe." Gordon handed her the dagger. "Now go and save the unicorn. If you reach your grandfather's grave, you are safe."

Mary Rose took the dagger and ran. She ran down the stairs, through the door, down to the courtyard. The horse lifted its head and looked at her surprised to see her in such a hurry. She didn't even bother saddling. She ran across the courtyard and whistled to call her horse to follow her. It came in a canter. But before they reached the big wooden entrance gate, it closed. Once more, they were trapped. Mary Rose wondered how Gordon could be there so quickly, but then she saw the grinning face of her cousin George in the window of the gate tower. They had been playing together as children and she knew, that he knew, that she knew, where the key was hidden. She would have to find another way. She looked around. A moment later, the door at the bottom of the clocktower opened and George stepped out. He held the key in his hand.

"Here is the key. Come and get it." He held a dagger in his hand. He wanted to fight.

Mary Rose took her dagger. She had fought against her cousin when she was young, when Gareth had taught them both the knightly skills. George had always hated fighting with a girl. He said a woman was not an equal opponent. But as Mary Rose became more experienced and more confident, she was able to beat him. She figured out that he was stronger, but a lot slower, and she learned to take advantage of this. She stepped towards George and they started to fight.

Gordon stepped out of the door and watched them fighting. Every now and then he shouted advice to them. Then he started strolling towards her horse that was standing a little way away from her now because it got nervous over the fighting. Mary Rose just clicked her tongue and the horse ran away out of reach of Gordon.

The fight was hard. Mary Rose realised that she had not practiced her fighting skills in years. And George was bigger and stronger than he used to be. Mary Rose knew she could not keep up this intensity, so she needed to end the fight as quickly as possible. She focused, and tried the three strikes she had developed to win against George, one after the other in quick succession. He managed to parry the first two, but the third came so fast that he lost his dagger. Mary Rose held her dagger against his neck.

"Give me the key."

He handed her the key, but attacked her in the same moment with his bare hands. Mary Rose managed to beat him back. She whistled and the horse came closer, but it was hesitant, made nervous by the fighting. She ran towards the horse and jumped on its bare back, and set off in a gallop towards the door. She turned the key in the lock and flung the door open. They set off across the bridge and into the pastures. Whilst she was racing with the horse over the bridge, she could already hear a second set of hooves behind her. Her uncle kept thoroughbreds. She knew her horse had no chance against a thoroughbred out on the open plain. She needed to find a route where the thoroughbred had to go slowly. Her grandfather's grave was on the other side of the bay, on the top of the cliff, from where one could see to the horizon over the ocean and all across the land of the family clan. There was a longer route across the plain, around the mountain, and a shorter path down the cliffs and along the bay.

Mary Rose chose the path down the cliffs and along the beach. At least on the downward slope of the rocky cliff path, the tall thoroughbred would have to slow right down. Along the sandy beach it would be able to catch up. But maybe, she could reach the cliff road at the other end of the bay before it had caught up. If she could reach the rocks first, she had won. The thoroughbred couldn't catch up on the rocky path uphill; there, her horse would be faster. It was smaller, more compact and very sure-footed. They would have a chance to make up some distance on the rocky ground.

The horse ran as fast as it could, but Mary Rose heard George getting closer.

"Run unicorn, run!" She encouraged the horse.

The tall, long-legged thoroughbred came closer in its big strides. George had caught up with her and he tried to push her horse away from its course towards the open plain. Mary Rose asked her horse to make a sudden stop, spin on its rear legs and race towards the entrance to the cliff road. The sudden stop and spin spooked the thoroughbred and it jumped to the side with a huge leap. George almost fell off. Whilst he was righting himself in the saddle, Mary Rose and her horse were approaching the entrance of the rocky path down to the beach. She looked over her shoulder when her horse walked around the first boulder. She saw George standing there, looking down at her and then up towards the mountain. He was obviously thinking about taking the route across the open plain. He would be able to let the thoroughbred run at full speed, but it was a longer way. And he would lose Mary Rose from his sight. Reluctantly, he asked the tall horse to follow his cousin down the rocky cliff path.

Mary Rose did not need to get off her horse when they walked underneath low hanging boulders, but she knew that George would have to dismount. Her horse walked on the rocky ground sure-footedly, and they made rapid progress. She hoped that the tall thoroughbred would not break its legs walking down from the cliffs. She looked back and she saw George and the thoroughbred stumbling around the first boulder. Meanwhile her horse settled into a steady, rhythmic walk down the steep path. It did not stumble once. It did not need to slow down much. It seemed to be happy and confident to walk on rocks. Mary Rose grew increasingly confident that they could make up enough ground now to reach the other side of the bay before the thoroughbred caught up. When she reached the sandy beach, she let her horse run as fast as it could. They dropped into a gallop along the beach. The wind was strong, the sea was wild and the waves were high. But her horse was reliable, and it went straight around the beach towards the other end of the bay.

Mary Rose looked back and she saw George and the thoroughbred finally reaching the beach. The first thing the tall horse did when it set a foot on the sand was to jump high into the air as a big wave hit the beach. This time George fell off. He was lucky that his head did not hit a boulder. He got up, but the horse had already set off in a gallop to escape the waves. All the same, Gordon's horses were trained well, and when George whistled, it came back. He climbed back on the horse and they raced along the beach. Mary Rose's horse could not match its pace. They were still some three hundred metres from the end of the beach when the thoroughbred caught up with them. This time George tried to push her off the horse.

'Nasty,' Mary Rose thought. He had a saddle on, and she didn't. She could not win a pushing match. She decided to lead her horse into the shallow water. The thoroughbred was still spooked by the waves and refused to come any closer. They were racing head to head, but George could not bring his horse close enough to push Mary Rose off her horse.

Then Mary Rose took the dagger carefully and slowly out of the belt, hoping George would not notice it. She knew, that George was not able to steer the thoroughbred without reins. Seizing an inattentive moment, when George was looking for the exit of the bay, she ran her dagger through one of his reins. With only one rein, George immediately lost control, and his horse began to run in circles. While he struggled, Mary Rose reached the exit of the bay, and her horse started to mount the rocky way uphill to the cliff. George was still trying to control his horse with only one rein. When Mary Rose was on top of the cliff, she let the horse drop into a canter. Just a few more strides up the hill, and there it was, her grandfather's grave.

Gordon was standing there, looking out to the sea. His long coat was blowing in the wind. One of his thoroughbreds was grazing nearby. He turned around and pulled his dagger.

"Old man, don't be stupid, it's a myth that drinking the blood of unicorns will make you live longer. Actually, I can promise you, that you will not live long enough to find out. If you don't leave my unicorn alone, I will have to kill you."

Mary Rose took a bow and an arrow from her back. It had been hidden underneath her riding hood. She shot an arrow into the ground by Gordon's feet.

"Go home, old man!"

"You are not able to kill a man, are you?"

"Maybe, but I will start by shooting an arrow into each of your legs, and then we can reassess the situation."

Mary Rose took the bow and arrow and aimed at Gordon's left leg.

"Why don't you take up a dagger fight with your old uncle?"

"I am not that stupid. I know its your best discipline. I am playing to my strengths as long as I make the rules."

"Very good: you win. Congratulations, you saved the last unicorn. You are a true knight of the unicorn."

Mary Rose smiled. She stroked the horse's neck and

got off its back. Then she and Gordon sat down at her grandfather's grave.

"He would have been very proud of you. You are an excellent rider. You managed to race your small horse against a thoroughbred. And you defeated your cousin in a dagger fight."

Mary Rose smiled. She was proud of herself.

THE FELLOWSHIP OF THE
UNICORN

*T*he wolf came towards Rosmarie with its tail wagging.

"Hello Rolf. Hello Frieda."

"Rosmarie! You scared me for a moment. I am glad it is you. What are you doing out here so early?"

"I found the tree circle and was curious to find out who could be the person that takes such a walk in the cold and dark, to come here and feed the animals. I must say, I am quite surprised it's you but also very proud."

Frieda smiled.

"Do you want to accompany me? You can take the snow mobile back up to the hut."

Rosmarie agreed and they started walking.

"How did you find the tree circle?"

"I followed the tracks of a deer. It led me there."

"A deer? I see."

Frieda nodded and she seemed to be in deep thought.

"I saw a big red one. Just for a couple of seconds, then

117

it disappeared. I was wondering about the story you used to tell me about the great hart. Can you tell me again what it was all about?"

"I think you are chosen to be the next witch of the valley. I was going to choose you. If the deer led you there, it chose you as well."

"What are you talking about grandma?"

"My dear Rosmarie, I want you to become the next woman who guards the mountain valley. There were always women who were guardians. Often they were dismissed as witches because they were strong and independent women. They could also heal with herbs and talk with animals. I honour the spirit of these women very much and I myself became one of them. It is a secret: the hidden lives of the guardians, witches, companions of the unicorn - whatever you want to call them. We must keep it secret because many of us were misunderstood, hunted down and killed. You never know. You must never talk about it with anyone. Except when you have chosen your successor, then you can tell her everything. That time has come for me now. I choose you as my successor."

"But Frieda! I don't know if I am ready for a big task like that and I don't know if I am strong enough for such a responsibility."

"You are. I know. You are destined to be a guardian. Just as your ancestresses were, and I as well."

"How did they know?"

"They were chosen by the spirits of the forest. One ancestress was chosen by an owl, another one by an ibex. I was chosen by the unicorn myself. But that was the last one we had. Since it disappeared, the deer is the guardian of the animals living up here. And the deer led you to the tree circle. You have been chosen."

Rosmarie felt proud that she had been chosen by the deer and her grandmother. Maybe her grandmother was right, maybe she was destined to be the next guardian. She had always admired the witches and those who walked with the unicorn and spoke to the animals. She wanted to be like that too. And what a surprise, to learn that her grandmother was such a guardian! Rosmarie was astounded. There were so many things she did not know about her grandmother.

"Tell me, how the unicorn chose you."

"One summer, when I was a young girl - it was during the war, before I married Viktor - my mother sent me up here to go foraging. There was not much food available at that time and the mushrooms, berries, herbs and roots of the forest were scarce and precious. People were hungry and many went foraging. I could not find anything in the lower highland forests. So I came all the way up here, close to the tree line. I crawled on all fours underneath some thick fir trees, hoping I might find some mushrooms there. The trees were so dense, that only a child or a slim person could get through. I saw a white horse grazing in a clearing. It looked at me. It saw straight into my heart and it lit a light inside me. I thought it must be a magic horse - a unicorn. I left and I never told anybody about it. That year winter came early, and snow fell in early September for the first time. I was worried about the horse. So I took some hay from our goats and sneaked up here whenever I thought there might be not enough to graze. Some time later a rumour was going through the valley.

Some people told stories that they had seen a witch and a unicorn. A border guard claimed that he had seen the witch and the unicorn in a foggy night and that they helped people escape across the mountain pass to Switzerland. So the soldiers went out to hunt the witch and the unicorn in the mountain forests. They said they killed them. I was very sad when I heard that. It is a shame that the last witch and the last unicorn were killed. I dreamt of the horse often. Again and again, it came to me in my dream. I could feel how it looked at me. I could feel how it touched my heart. I could feel the light. Then I realised that I was the one who was chosen by the unicorn to take the witch's place as the human guardian of the valley. I had always admired the women who risked their lives and sacrificed themselves to do what they thought was right, regardless of any conventions, law or orders. I thought I would never be that brave. But since the encounter with the unicorn, I felt stronger and braver than ever before. I just did what I felt was the right thing to do, regardless of what my husband, the mayor or the priest, the police or the soldiers expected. Ever since, I have come here to feed the animals when it is really cold and there is no food for them. I try to protect them and the valley as much as I can. I help anybody who is kind, honest and brave, without expecting anything in return. I am the witch, as some people would call it, or if you prefer, I am the sorceress of the unicorn. And you are the next one. The spirit lives on."

Rosmarie was surprised about what her grandmother told her. She felt very proud to be a Sorceress of the Unicorn. She felt that maybe it was the task she was meant to fulfil. She had always felt called to do big deeds. This was her chance. Even though, she had doubts as well, she wanted to be the chosen one, she wanted to be a guardian, she wanted to be a witch and most of all, she wanted to be a sorceress of the unicorn and join its fellowship and preserve its spirit. She had had dreams about a white horse since she was little. That must have been a sign. The unicorn was calling her to become a guardian. Now she knew.

A few days later, she had another five o'clock rendezvous with Frieda. She sneaked out of the house and looked around several times to make sure nobody was following her. She needed to protect the secret. She met her grandmother at the boulder, and they swept away their tracks as they climbed it. They crawled underneath the trees, and stood together in the circle. Frieda laid down the gifts in several small heaps of hay, and put some sunflower seeds and oats out as well. Then she knelt down. Rosmarie could not believe it but immediately birds, squirrels and rabbits appeared. It was magical to watch Frieda kneeling there motionless surrounded by the creatures of the forest. After a while, two roe deer joined them, and finally a big red deer entered the circle.

Rosmarie was happy. Suddenly she was living in a fairy tale. Her grandmother had a secret life as a witch, and had chosen her as the next guardian. Her grandmother was friends with the animals in the forest. She had taken on the duty to guard over the valley and all that lived in the forest after the last unicorn had disappeared. The fellowship of the unicorn kept its spirit alive and it would always live on.

NIGHTMARES

Tomorrow would be the day. In the morning, Mary Rose would start out on her mission. She had packed everything and checked everything three times. She had checked the horse several times today. She had studied the maps and had called up all the stables where she and her horse would find shelter for the nights. She had checked the ferry across the channel. She went through the list of things she must not forget one more time. So finally, she sat down. She took her grandmother's travel diary and opened it at a random page.

At the marketplace the horse dealers offered me a lot of money for the horse.

"Don't be silly," they said. "You will be rich. Give us the horse."

I knew they would sell her for good money to the army. And she would be sent to war. She would be worked to death or torn to pieces by the bombs. I just could not sell her. She saved me. I owed her my life. They were right, I needed money and I had no idea how to go on. But I could not give this amazing horse to those men. So I rode off.

As I left the villages behind and entered the forest, the horse signalled that something was behind us. I had a feeling that the horse dealers might be also horse-thieves and that they might try to steal my horse. When we came to a stream I had an idea to trick the thief. I rode into the water and out on the other side. Then I made her go backwards back into the water. The tracks at the riverbank looked like we had left the river on the other side. Instead I rode down the river. The plan worked out. Nobody followed us anymore. From then on we stayed in forests and hid. One day the horse wallowed in a muddy puddle and its coat was covered with dirt and it looked greyish-brown afterwards. I left the dirt on, since I hoped the mud crust would hide her from the greedy eyes of the horse dealers. I made sure she was always as dirty as possible and her mane was tousled.

Mary Rose put the book down.

'Wow,' she thought. 'Grandma was really incorruptible. Even though she was in an emergency situation, she did not sell the horse. But yet, she already knew the horse was worth a fortune, but more than this, it was life-saving for her.'

Mary Rose could not imagine what her grandmother had gone through. Somehow it made her feel cowardly because she was scared and worried about her journey even though it was a time of peace and wealth. She had saved money, she had a satnav, a mobile phone, and she had places to stay for the nights. And still, it was somehow scary to ride into an uncertain future and to be out there all alone. Her biggest worry was of course that the horse would get injured. She had dreamed about it, and woken abruptly in a cold sweat. If the horse was spooked by a car and jumped aside, and hurt its leg, this could already be the end of the journey. If it stepped into a hole in the ground, it could break its leg. What if they had bad hay at the horse stables or farms and the horse had a colic? It was one of her recurring nightmares that she came to the stable and the horse was lying on the ground, sweating, in pain. She worried about the ferry-ride. She had a nightmare, she dreamt that someone scared the horse, it reared, tore the rope and ran off. It jumped over the fence into the water. She woke up, soaked in sweat. She had another nightmare where she crossed the train-tracks and the horse got stuck with its hoof and the train came. She woke up with panicking eyes when she heard the horn. Finally, she had that nightmare where she came to the stable in the morning and the horse was not there anymore.

There were a million things that could happen. It was a great responsibility to be entrusted with a horse. She was responsible for its wellbeing. She knew that this responsibility was what made her worry. She needed to know about the dangers for a horse and try to eliminate them in advance. That was the task of the horsewoman, the knight. She feared to fail and disappoint herself. She could never forgive herself if something happened to the horse that she should have seen coming. But she also feared disappointing her grandmother and her grandfa-ther - even though he was not alive anymore - both of whom had always believed in her. It would be humiliating for her having to admit that her parents were right, it was too dangerous and she had been recklessly risking her horse's life. But most of all, she was responsible to the horse. If a horse followed her voluntarily, it chose her as its leader and it put its life in her hands. It was a great responsibility to be responsible for the life of another living being.

Mary Rose tried to calm down. She wanted to think of something nice instead of her nightmares. She needed to focus on something positive. So she took her diary and started writing.

The amazing thing about horses is their uncompromising loyalty to their herd, their family, their friends. If you win the trust and respect of a horse - for that you have to prove your trustworthiness, reliability and your loyalty - then you can count on the horse in any situation. It will never let you down. It will carry you across mountains, rivers, endless plains, without ever leaving you behind. It will hold together when all seems lost. It will keep going when you give up. It will make you fly and it will make you rise again when you fall. It will show you that you are stronger than you know. It will show you a world where friendship never ends. It will turn your world around and turn your worldview upside down. It will open your eyes and you will see the world in a new light. And suddenly you realise that the one friend in your life who never let you down is a horse.

Mary Rose closed the diary. 'I am a poet,' she thought. 'I write beautiful horse poetry.' For a moment she felt better. But in the next second her worries came back. But what if she lost her path? No, she would find it. She needed to trust. But what if the horse got injured and she could not continue riding? No, nothing would happen to the horse. But what if she travelled all the way and then she could not find the one woman she was looking for? What if she was already dead? Her grandmother was old and in very good shape but what if the other woman had already passed away? What if she did not want the gift? What would she do then? Then she would call her grandmother and ask her what to do. There was no point going crazy over all of these things now. If she did not find the woman, at least she had tried. She could not control whether or not the woman was alive. But she would do everything she could do to find her.

Mary Rose could not sleep. Now she sat at the window and looked out into the night. She was excited and nervous, happy and worried, hopeful and anxious. She was strong, and yet she felt the weight of expectations. She was tired, but too excited to sleep.

Mary Rose went outside into the night. She walked a few steps. The night was mild and the sky was clear. The horses stood outside their shed and watched her. One of them - the one she would take on the mission - came towards her. The horse gently blew its breath at her hand as if to say:

"It will be all right, don't worry. I am with you."

She gave the horse a hug. "Thank you," she said.

She looked up at the stars and the moon. In the moment she looked up to the sky she saw a shooting star. Her grandmother had always told her, shooting stars carry wishes away with them to the sky and when a new star is born on the night sky, the wish becomes true.

So she wished for the strength to complete the mission and fulfil her grandmother's last wish.

She sat in silence for a while and looked at the stars. The sky was clear, there was not a single cloud. In the distance she could hear the waves breaking on the cliffs. She wondered if the woman who saved her grandmother was looking at the stars as well. She felt connected to her in a way.

"I am coming," she said out loud. "I will come and find you soon. Please await our arrival."

Then she walked towards the horse that was grazing nearby. She climbed onto its back and rode slowly towards the coast. She wanted to say goodbye to the sea and the land that she called her home. The night was dark but starlit. The wind blew through her hair and the horse's mane was blowing in the wind. When they reached the hilltop they stopped. They just stood there and took a deep breath. The air smelled of the salty sea and the mossy heath. The land was quiet and dark. The sea was black and moving, and just underneath the moon it glittered in the moonlight. The night sky opened above the beautiful scenery.

They stayed for a while and then returned to the cottage. She said good night to the horses and she went inside, fell into her bed, and at last she fell asleep.

THE DREAM

*T*hat night, Rosmarie had an unusual dream. She dreamt about a faraway landscape somewhere she had never been. It was an impressive sight, with mountains and lakes - or was it the sea? It was rough, there was a harsh wind blowing and the grassland was meagre with very few trees. She dreamt of a young woman - she might be about her age. She spoke to her. She could not understand the words she was saying. It sounded like a foreign language. The wind was howling, so she could not hear the words properly. But somehow she knew that the woman spoke to her. Somehow, she knew, that the woman spoke to her in her dream.

Rosmarie was curious, because she knew that this woman wanted to tell her something. But it also frustrated her, because she could not understand what she was saying. And somehow she knew that the woman had an important message for her. She tried as hard as she could to listen, but she could not understand a word she said. She could only hear a humming in the wind.

Then, suddenly the woman turned around and walked off. She walked across a field and at the horizon was the sea. She could see her walking through the grass, her hair blowing in the wind. She walked towards a white horse and touched it gently. Then she climbed on the back of the horse. They set off towards the horizon. The wind was still blowing. Their silhouettes got smaller as they disappeared into the night.

Wide awake, Rosmarie sat up in her bed with her heart racing. The dream had been so vivid. Who was this woman? Where was she? And why did she appear in Rosmarie's dream? What did she have to say to Rosmarie? Rosmarie was still disappointed at not being able to hear the woman's message.

Rosmarie tried to calm herself. She sighed. She took a few deep breaths. Then she got up and opened the window. She looked up at the stars and the moon. It was a beautiful starlit night. She closed her eyes, collected her thoughts, and put both hands on her heart. Then she spoke out loudly into the night.

"Dear woman, whoever you are. Thank you for coming to me in my dream. I know that you have something important to say to me. Unfortunately, I could not understand what you said. Please repeat the message for me. I am waiting. I am listening."

After she had said it, she felt better. She did not know if the woman would receive the message - she did not even know if she existed at all - but she hoped that if it was important she would return in a dream and would say it again. By now Rosmarie was wide awake. Where was this place she had dreamt of? Her father had explained to her that in dreams, the brain processed experiences of the day. But then how was it possible that she dreamt about a place she had never been or seen before, and a woman she had never met?

She took out her laptop and began a little research. The internet connection up here in the mountains was very slow, so it took her a while. But eventually, she read an article about dream research that confirmed what her father had told her. Then she read an article, which was not scientific but spiritual, claiming that through dreams it was possible to communicate with other beings that one was connected to - sometimes without even knowing. It said that through dreams, feelings, and pictures, it was possible for a spiritual person to communicate with other spirits - the deceased, animals, and other entangled souls, and soulmates. Rosmarie liked this idea, even though she was not sure if it was really possible. She set about searching for pictures of coastlines. She looked at hundreds of pictures, but she could not find one that looked enough like the place in her dream. In time she grew frustrated, and her head began to ache, as she grew more impatient with the slow connection. So she put the computer to one side and tried to sleep again.

However, Rosmarie could still not switch her mind off. She lay in bed and looked at the ceiling. The woman, the horse, and the strange land would not leave her mind. She got up again, lit a candle, and started drawing. She tried to draw what she had seen. She drew the landscape, the rough heathland, the shores, the sea, the sky, the moon, the stars, and a woman on a white horse following their path through the night. It was such a fascinating landscape, a rocky, yet green mountain leading to a sandy beach. The wind was strong and the landscape rough. It did not seem mediterranean, she thought, it must be somewhere up north.

'Tomorrow I will do another search in my lunch break,' she thought.

She needed to sleep now. She had to start working early tomorrow and she would be very tired if she did not get any sleep. But on the other hand, it was a starlit new moon night and she had had a captivating dream. Maybe she was not meant to sleep tonight? She remembered that she had once read a poem saying that if you cannot sleep, it is because you are awake in someone else's dream. She liked that idea. She often had trouble getting to sleep, especially when the moon was full. The quote helped her to stay relaxed and not get upset if she could not fall asleep. She liked the thought that somebody else was dreaming of her.

Finally, she gave up on trying to get back to sleep. She dressed quickly and quietly, then she sneaked out of the house. The night was dark. Up here in the mountains the nights felt even darker than elsewhere. However, something was calling her out into the dark forest. She did not know why, but she suddenly felt like she had to go out into the forest tonight. She had never been actually scared of the dark. She loved the nights. She liked to sit on the roof and look at the stars. She liked the dark and the moonlight. She liked the silence at night. But going out into the forest at night was something else.

Rosmarie suddenly felt a creeping fear, now that she was standing outside the house in the dark and cold night. The longer she stood out there, the more she felt that the idea to head out into the forest, alone, in the dark and in the cold, had been a bad one. But she did not want to go back either. She stood there and watched the mountain scenery at night, covered by snow. There was sometimes snow in early spring up here. The snow made the night less dark. Rosmarie took a deep breath, summoned all her courage, and stepped out into the dark. She walked towards the forest.

THE JOURNEY BEGINS

*M*ary Rose woke up early. It was six o'clock. She got up immediately and went outside to look after the horses. They had already left the shed and were grazing on the pasture. Two of them lifted their heads for a moment, whinnied a greeting and continued grazing. One of them stopped grazing and looked at her. It knew. Mary Rose went up to the horse.

"You know that we are going on a journey. The time has come. Say goodbye to your friends."

She gave the horse an extra portion of oats and hay and went back inside to make breakfast. Grandmother Annemarie was up early too. Mary Rose's stomach got more and more upset as the nervousness rose. But she still ate as much as she could because she did not want to start out on her journey hungry.

Then she put the saddle and bags on her horse. She checked the legs and hooves of the horse again. Finally they were ready to leave! Mary Rose went to her grandmother, who was sitting on a bench in front of the cottage. She gave her a long hug.

"I love you. Take care of yourself. Call uncle Gordon if you need anything."

"I love you too. You take care of yourself and your horse. I will be with you in my thoughts."

They both had tears in their eyes. It was a hard goodbye for Mary Rose because she did not even know if she would see her grandmother again. But she stayed strong, she got on her horse and started riding away. She turned around in the saddle and waved goodbye to her grandmother. She was waving back.

The other horses whinnied but they stayed with grandmother Annemarie. The horses knew. Mary Rose was fascinated by the horses every time anew. They seemed to know. They sensed what was going on. They seemed to be able to accept the course of life. The horse walked off confidently whilst Mary Rose was struggling. But she knew that the horse knew it might leave this place forever and may never return. Yet it seemed to have less of a struggle than Mary Rose. The tears were running across Mary Rose's face as she thought that she might just have said goodbye forever to her grandmother. It was hard for her to leave this place.

From the top of the hill she could see the manor. Uncle Gordon and her cousin George rode with two of the tall brown horses towards her. When they came up to her Gordon said:

"We give you an escort across the main road and the bridge. Just to make sure you set across safely!"

Mary Rose smiled. Great! The bridge was dangerous

to cross. Some drivers were inconsiderate and if the horse got nervous she could not get off anywhere. She was glad about the escort. They crossed the bridge safely and said good-bye. Suddenly a car stopped and her parents got out of the car. They had come all the way from London in the early morning hours to wish her good luck. Mary Rose was touched. All of them waved her good-bye as she rode off across the hills.

The horse fell into a rhythmic walk and carried her safely. Mary Rose was overwhelmed with feelings. She cried because it was hard for her to let go. It took a while until Mary Rose could stop crying and could see clearly again. She took a deep breath. She looked at the beautiful landscape and tried to enjoy the ride, but she could not quite manage it. Her stomach was turning and her heart was aching. It broke her heart to leave her grandmother at this age and yet she did it for her grandmother because it was her final wish. It also felt like she was torn in two, between the desire to stay in the peace and safety of her home on the one side, and the will to complete her mission, experience an adventure, and find her purpose on the other.

Mary Rose shook her head. She was trying to shake off the emotions and get focused. She took a few deep breaths and asked the horse for a slow trot. Trotting was good. Mary Rose concentrated more on the ride, the path and the rhythmic trot of the horse, trying not to think of her home disappearing behind the hills. She fell into a trance. There was nothing but the rhythmic trot of the horse. They were trotting through the beautiful landscape of Scotland. The horse was white, the hills were green, the sea was deep blue, and the sky was clear.

It was as if the only things that existed were she and her horse, trotting through Scotland. Every now and then they crossed a street or they had to get through a gate. Then they continued their trot. It was as if the rhythmic shaking of the trotting horse and the stunning beauty of the landscape shook the pain away and led Mary Rose into a state of presence of mind and acceptance. Maybe, it was the magic of the unicorn spreading to its rider. Nevertheless, somehow it soothed the pain and calmed her. The tears dried up, and she started to enjoy the wind on her face.

The horse trotted with an even rhythm. It went up and down the hills, without ever losing its pulse. Mary Rose was always astounded how enduring horses were. She had taken many three day rides in preparation for the journey, and in the last summer she had even taken a week-long trekking ride. Even so, she found it remark-able that it kept its speed, its gait, its direction and its rhythm for hours. So far Mary Rose had not needed to take her compass out, nor she had to reach for the satnav. The horse found the way all by itself. Did it know where they were heading?

The horse kept its course without hesitation, without doubt, as if it were the most natural thing at all. Mary Rose remembered the last chapter of grandmother Annemarie's diary, in which the horse had taken the lead and had kept going unerringly. It led her grandmother to the beautiful Scottish headland, straight into the arms of her future husband. Was that all a coincidence? Grand-mother Annemarie did not believe in coincidences. She believed in the senses of her magic horse that seemed to know where she needed to go. Well, this horse was a descendant of grandmother Annemarie's horse. Maybe this ability, sensitivity, these magic powers were inheritable among horses? In any case, this one seemed to know that it had a mission to fulfill and was trotting confidently towards their destination.

'If I had known that the horse would know the way, I would not have spent day after day looking at maps and planning routes,' Mary Rose thought.

Nevertheless, she was glad that she was well prepared. She was a knight. She was smart, thoughtful and always had a thought-out plan. She sighed. She managed to relax a little bit. Things were going well so far. After a while, she asked the horse to walk. Once it was cooled down completely, she got off, took the saddle and bridle off, and let it graze for a while. She lay down in the grass and watched the horse. It was grazing and it seemed to be relaxed. It still behaved as if it were a perfectly normal thing to leave behind their home, their family, their country, and ride towards an uncertain destiny. The grass seemed to taste here just as good as it did at home. After a while, the horse was indicating that it wanted to move again. Mary Rose put the saddle on the horse and followed it as it walked off. To her it seemed it was heading slightly off the route, but she let it go where it wanted to go and followed it. After a few minutes, they reached a stream where the horse drank and Mary Rose filled her bottle. Then they continued their path.

The horse walked up and down countless hills. The landscape changed slightly, but still Mary Rose knew the area well. When they reached a hilltop, she could see the stud of uncle Gordon's friend Mr O'Connor and his son

Brian. This was where they planned to spend their first night. They had made their daily distance. Dusk was falling and their place to stay was in sight. She let the horse stroll as slowly as it liked. It stopped here and there and grabbed some grass. Before darkness fell, they reached the farmstead. Mary Rose was happy, that they had managed to complete the first day of their journey without any incident and in time. That was good.

GUARDIANS

*T*he night was starlit. The silhouette of the majestic peaks reached high up into the sky, the crescent moon just above. Rosmarie was wandering through the night. She walked along the path towards the forest. She did not really know where she was going. She had just had a dream and she somehow felt like she might have inherited some talents she had not known about from one of her ancestresses, who were witches and guardians of the valley. Now that she knew that her grandmother was one of them and she had decided that she wanted to follow in her footsteps, she felt something calling her out into the dark forest. So she went out under the new moon on this cold early spring night to look in the darkness for - she did not know what for. But it did not matter. She would find out.

The forest was different at night. It was dark and shadowy, and here and there a shaft of light shone through to allow a guess of the shapes of the trees. The light revealed only one side of the silhouettes of the tree-trunks. It was beautiful but also unnerving. Luckily, the snow on the ground made the forest floor brighter and she could at least see where she was stepping. She saw a shadow flit past. Was it a fox? An owl startled her when it flew off a branch nearby. It was a little bit spooky to be alone in the wood. Suddenly, a loud noise reverberated from the rock walls on the opposite mountain range. Was that a gunshot? Rosmarie froze. Then she heard the beating of wings, and she saw shadows of animals running through the forest for cover.

Rosmarie was terrified. But she decided that she had to see what was going on. After all, she was going to be the next guardian. She sneaked in the direction from where the shot had come from. She had a suspicion that it was from the raised stand of the huntsman. The huntsman, who had come after her grandfather, was a man who hunted for trophies, he was not a man who chose this work because he cared for the wildlife. It was spring, and a long way off hunting season. Rosmarie knew it was illegal to shoot animals in spring.

Suddenly, the big red stag stood in front of her. It looked into her eyes. Rosmarie stood still and returned its gaze. How beautiful its eyes were. What a wonderful creature! As the deer walked off slowly, Rosmarie saw it leaving a trail of red blood in the snow.

'Oh no!' she thought. 'Not the deer! Huntsman, you are a nasty man. I will hold you to account for this!'

Rosmarie took a branch and swept away the tracks of the deer. Then she ran back to the hut as fast as she could, stumbling over roots and slipping on the snowy ground. A branch scratched her face, but she kept running. When she entered the hut, she grabbed her mobile phone, a leg from a stuffed deer in the huntsmen's chamber in the restaurant, and a big bottle of ketchup. As she ran back towards the door, she saw the mask of the Knecht Ruprecht - a scary fellow of St. Nicholas in regional folklore - hanging on the wall next to the stuffed head of a deer. She grabbed it and ran back outside. On the way she called Frieda. She gasped into the phone:

"The huntsman shot the deer. I need to save it. Help me."

She hung up and ran back up to the spot where she had met the deer. Her heart was beating heavily and her lung hurt from breathing in the ice-cold air while she was running. But she had no time to rest. She had to act quickly. Using the stuffed leg she made a new track leading in the other direction and she threw some ketchup into the snow every few steps. She wiped away her own tracks carefully as she went. She forged a new trail down to the main road. There Rosmarie's own footprints became indistinguishable from the others.

She led the track down the road, and a way down she turned off towards the ravine. Under a huge, overhanging rock, she hid. She put on the mask of Knecht Ruprecht, pulled up the hood of her coat, and climbed up onto a big stone to make herself appear bigger. She put her phone on a ledge in the rock and set it to record, just in case. Then she waited. She was nervous and anxious. She had to hope that the huntsman would not shoot her.

Just a second later, she heard steps coming closer. The huntsman appeared right in front of her. He froze

the moment he saw her and he stared at her unbelievingly.

She spoke with her loudest and deepest voice:
"Huntsman, you have violated the local hunting laws and
shot a deer during closed season. You are a bad man and
you will pay for that. I am the witch of the forest, and the
deer is under my protection. Now run for your life!"

Rosmarie shouted the last words with all the fury
that arose in her heart. Her voice was loud and echoed in
the hollow underneath the rock, as if the very rocks
were repeating the threat, as it reverberated through the
whole valley: "Run for your life! Life! Life!"

The huntsman stumbled backwards and fell over a
root on the ground. He got back on his feet and he ran
off without looking back. He did not know what was
going on. A mysterious figure threatened him in the
midst of the night. He ran for his life. He did not know
what he had seen - a demon? A witch? In any case, it
knew that he had fired a shot in closed season. He had
been after this deer for years, but it was too clever so he
had never had a chance for a shot. But tonight it had
come close so he wanted to take his chance. It had been a
mistake. He had regretted it in the same moment. He
realised as he took the shot, he would not kill his target.
The deer had not gone down, but it had taken off. He
had sworn bitterly and cursed this deer. But he really
prized its antlers, the biggest he had ever seen. Then -
the demon, the witch appeared before him.

The huntsman ran, out of his mind with fear. He was
not superstitious, but this encounter had seemed far
more real than he could handle. The people had always
spoken about stories of the witches that lived up here.

Were they true? He had always thought they were just sagas and superstition. But he was sure he had just seen a big demon in long robes, with a scary horned face and the creaking voice of a witch. He ran, even though the ice cold air hurt in his lungs. Then he stopped.

There was a wolf standing right in front of him. It snarled and bared its teeth. He froze in fear. What could he do? The wolf was close enough to pounce on him. He would not have time to aim his rifle. Could this night get any worse? In the same moment, he noticed a shadowy figure in a long coat and faceless black hood standing beneath the trees.

"Huntsman, you are a bad man. You shot a deer during closed season. You shall pay for that. The witches of the forest do not accept behaviour like yours. If you don't mend your ways and become a better person, fate will take its revenge for what you do to other creatures."

The wolf was still baring its teeth. The huntsman was at the edge of insanity now. He was terrified. He surrendered.

"I am sorry. Forgive me. I will become a better person. I will try harder. But please do not put a curse on me!"

"You have put the curse on yourself. You shot the oldest spirit of this forest. If it dies, the demons will take revenge."

"I am sorry. I made a mistake. What can I do?"

"Become a better person. Do not try. Do it."

The huntsman whimpered. "I promise. I will."

The wolf disappeared with one massive leap into the darkness. When he looked towards the witch again, it had disappeared. He shook his head in disbelief. Then he started walking. He prayed that the deer would not die. He was not superstitious at all, but after this night, he was scared that maybe there were spirits, witches, and demons out there after all. And he had upset them. They were protecting the valley. He had been greedy. He had shot the oldest spirit of the forest, just because he wanted to have its antlers and impress his fellow hunters. Could he ever make up for what he had done? No, if the deer died, that was it. The demons would chase him. And he deserved it.

TRAIL OF MAGIC

he next morning, Mary Rose got up before sunrise. She went straight to the stables and attended to her horse. Brian had already fed it and now he was grooming a tall thoroughbred. Mary Rose thanked him. The horse seemed happy and ate its hay. Brian leaned next to Mary Rose and they watched the horses chewing their hay for a while.

Then he smiled at her and said: "Let's get some breakfast."

They went to the house and ate heartily. Mr O'Connor looked at Mary Rose for a moment before he said: "Gordon told me you are a very good horse-trainer, just as your grandfather. I was wondering if you could look at one of our horses that is very difficult to handle. We had the vet look at it and various horse-trainers. Nothing helped so far."

Mary Rose's face lit up. "Yes, certainly. I will look at it."

After breakfast, they returned to the stable and showed Mary Rose the horse they had problems with. Mary Rose observed the horse and its trainer for a while. She had the feeling that the horse did not trust humans since it looked stressed all the time and she had the feeling it never got the time it would have needed to start trusting. She gave Brian some exercises he should practice with the horse until she came back. To begin with, he should open the door of the box and just stand there and wait until the horse came to him, instead of rushing in and chasing the horse with the halter. Then he should touch the horse everywhere, legs and ears and only when he could do that without any problem, he should put the halter on. Even if it took a long time, he must not take the next step before. Then he should bring it to the round-pen and work with it at liberty, without using a rope. He should be able to make the horse stop and go with just a gesture. The horse should come to him when he invited it and he should be able to send it out again. Mary Rose demonstrated with her horse how it should look like. Mr O'Connor and Brian were impressed of her demonstration of Liberty Training. The horse was entirely free and responded to almost invisible gestures.

Mr O'Connor shook her hand and said: "You have the job. I am impressed. Your uncle was right. You are a gifted horsewoman."

Mary Rose smiled, thanked him and then she prepared for the ride. Brian came with the tall brown thoroughbred that he had been brushing. Mary Rose thanked him for everything, and then got on her horse.

Brian watched her for a moment and then he said: "I was wondering if you would allow me to accompany you for a little bit?"

Mary Rose looked at him surprised. She had assumed he was heading to the race track. He smiled at her. Indeed, Mary Rose had to admit, that his company was very pleasant, and courteous.

She agreed. "You can accompany me for half a day's ride."

They started to ride side by side. The morning air was cold and fresh, and there was a thick fog sitting over the land. They rode in silence for a while.

"I like your approach. The exercises you gave me to practice are the opposite of what we do usually. We rush into the box, put the stuff on the horse and take them to the track where we make them run as fast as they can," Brian said.

"And that is the problem. Horses are very attentive. They watch you and see everything. You are speaking to them with every move you make. They don't take you by your word, they judge you by your actions. The way you treat them tells them what kind of man you are and what sort of relationship you are seeking to establish. If you rush in and out instead of being present and in the moment, if you drag them instead of allowing them to choose to follow, if you push them instead of giving them the time it takes, if you hunt and catch them instead of waiting for them to seek you, then you are telling them you are not making the effort to build a real partnership."

"Wow," Brian was baffled. "That's quite hard to take.

But I can see your point. From the horses' perspective it is pushy and hasty. I will keep it in mind. Thanks for the advice."

They rode in silence most of the day and it was a pleasant feeling. Mary Rose enjoyed his company and she felt it was good that they enjoyed the ride and just being there in each other's company, without having to talk constantly. She had the feeling they understood each other quite tacitly. From time to time, she was aware of Brian looking at her. The horses walked side by side and kept each other's pace. They admired the beauty of the morning, the fresh air and every once in a while, they gave each other a smile. Midday crept up on them quickly, and she almost felt sorry that she could not enjoy being with him any longer. But she had a journey ahead of her she needed to make on her own.

Right in this moment Brian spoke out loud: "There is something about you and your horse. I don't know what it is, but I just can't take my eyes off you. You both - together - you are just wonderful. I mean you are both beautiful, but it is more than that, it is this feeling one has, if one looks at you."

He stopped speaking and watched Mary Rose. Maybe he was trying to find out if he was pushing it too far or if he could carry on.

Mary Rose gave him a gentle smile. "Thank you," she said. She was truly charmed. She had never gotten such a compliment from a man before. For her, it was touching as he had opened up to her. He also showed that he could sense the connection of her and her horse. Even though he did not yet have a name for it.

"I know you have to go your way so I won't hold you back. But take care. I am looking forward to see you when you come back. I wish you the best of luck," he said. Then he smiled at her and waved just once with his hand. He then turned his horse and headed back.

Mary Rose was charmed. He recognised her and he respected her plans and decisions without trying to change them. That was honourable, recognising that she had a mission to complete, a purpose to serve, a path to find. On top of that, Mary Rose felt good about the job offer of Mr O'Connor. That was the first job offer she got since her grandfather's death. And it was a big job. Mr O'Connor's horses were very valuable. If she would do a good job, then she would gain a reputation that would bring her more clients.

Somehow it filled her with a vibrant feeling of self-esteem. Her horse seemed to be able to feel the change in her mood, and it seemed to walk even more light-footedly than usual. It seemed to prance on the clouds. The sunshine made its fur glow.

She rode down the path through a village. It was a pretty countryside village. Along the main road all the houses were painted in bright pastel colours. Many people were on the street since it was Saturday and there was a food market. People stopped and watched them in awe. It seemed that they could not take their eyes off her and her horse. Wherever they went, people seemed to be captivated by the gracefulness of the horse and the young woman.

Mary Rose gently stroked the neck of her horse. Once more she realised, how lucky she was. Everybody -

literally everybody - even the teenage boys, who pretended to not be interested in horses - stood still in admiration, the moment when they spotted the horse and Mary Rose. Mary Rose felt proud and at the same time she was overwhelmed with feelings of gratitude.

"We are magical! There must be something magical about us. Look at the people staring at us and watching us with their mouths open. They probably have never seen a unicorn before! It seems like we are leaving a trail of magic everywhere we go!" Mary Rose said to her horse.

The horse whinnied and it shook its head so that its long mane blew in the wind. It shone white, with a golden and silver touch in the sun. It looked truly like it came from a fairy tale.

Mary Rose liked the idea of bringing magic and bliss to the people. She wanted to enchant the world with some unicorn dust, charm, and fascination. People did not believe in fairytales. They did not tell their children magical stories anymore. People had forgotten about unicorns. They were merely beasts on ancient coats of arms, derived from old myths. They could not imagine that unicorns were actually real! They could not imagine that once wild horses roamed the land and enchanted the world with their spirit, their beauty, their gracefulness. They did not know what Mary Rose knew: unicorns are real.

The unicorns needed to come back and enchant the world again. That was their purpose. They were bringers of light, saviours of hope, healers of the living. They awakened the sense of enchantment and a deep consciousness for the beauty of life. Mary Rose knew this, thus it was important that she travelled by horse. She imagined how she and her horse left a glittering track of unicorn dust as they rode across the land. Everybody who saw it was enchanted straight away and could suddenly see and feel magic wherever they went.

THE SECRET LIVES OF WOMEN

*T*he deer was lying at the bottom of the rock wall. Rosmarie and Frieda had carefully wiped away its tracks.

"I think we need a doctor," Rosmarie said. "Shall I call mum?"

Frieda nodded.

Rosmarie called her mother, who was a veterinarian. She told her that they needed her immediately. Rosmarie stayed with the deer and tried to stop the bleeding. Frieda went back down to pick up her daughter Viktoria. As they came back, the dawn was breaking. When Viktoria saw the deer, she kneeled down beside it and took its head. The deer let her stroke its forehead.

"Red Dawn," Viktoria whispered.

A tear ran across her cheek. She hugged the deer, and to Rosmarie's surprise, this shy animal seemed to lean into her arms returning her embrace with its long neck and big head. After they released each other, Viktoria inspected the wound.

"Do you two know each other?" Frieda asked her daughter.

"Um, yes, we do."

Frieda nodded with a contented smile on her face. "Is this the stag you raised that summer you spent in the highlands herding goats?"

Viktoria looked at Frieda with surprise.

"You knew about that?"

Frieda smiled knowingly. "I was very proud of you. You were such a young girl with such a big heart and you were extraordinarily brave."

Viktoria looked at Frieda. She was completely baffled. "Thank you," she mumbled. "I didn't know you knew. If I had known, I could have asked for your help. That would have made things much easier for me."

"I know. But I knew you could manage it yourself. It was a great experience for you. I was there in spirit, giving you my backing. But you managed it all on your own. That was great."

Viktoria still seemed baffled, but she went to work without any further word. She cut the bullet out. The deer kept still throughout the operation. The bullet was easy to remove but the deer had lost a lot of blood. Viktoria was not sure if it would survive. She was very sad. She sat by its side and stroked it. Rosmarie and Frieda brought hay and straw for it to lie on and to keep it warm. When the day dawned Viktoria decided to stay with the deer. She called her clinic and asked the other veterinarian to cover for her.

Luckily, the coming days were warm and all the snow

melted, taking away the tracks, the traces of blood and ketchup. Spring was coming. That was good. The deer was very weak. It needed care and was very vulnerable in its weakened condition, even the foxes could be dangerous for it in this state. On top of that, Frieda had seen a lone wolf in the forest, when she went foraging the previous spring. That was a while ago, but it could still be around. Rosmarie wanted to protect the great hart.

She decided to build a hut at the bottom of the rock wall and stay there as long as the deer needed care. During her afternoon breaks, she constructed a hut with branches from the forest. She made a bed of leaves and dried moss. She carried many branches up there and built a cocoon that felt nice and cosy. Frieda brought more hay and straw every time she came to visit. Soon, there was a nice bed for the deer and a cosy enclosure for the people. Rosmarie was content with the construction. Its walls made from branches, leaves, moss and straw, were dense, and they kept the wind and the cold out nicely. At the same time, the cocoon was in a dry spot underneath the overhanging rocks sheltered from the rain, except on those days when the storm lashed the rain horizontally across the landscape. To the other side, protection was given by a steep, slanted hill with a dense fir tree forest. It was a protected and comfortable space up here. From the cocoon she could see the deer, lying on a bed of hay and straw nearby. She kept some distance because it was a wild animal and should stay that way. The only person that was allowed to come close was Viktoria. She was its foster mother.

At night, Rosmarie locked the door of her room from

the inside and climbed out of the window. Then she sneaked out into the forest. She walked down the trail and went up the steep hill to the rock wall. The deer was still very weak and spent all its time lying down. She fed it, and cleaned its wound. She watched over the deer all night, but did not get much sleep herself. She was scared out there alone in the dark and she was startled by every noise. Frieda said, that was normal and good since she was in the wilderness, she needed to be alert all the time, even when she was sleeping. That was crucial for survival in the wild forest.

Viktoria and Frieda came by regularly. They took it in turns to nurse the deer. Frieda came every day to bring hay and straw, change its bandage and give it medicine. Viktoria came as often as she could. By the weekend, both Viktoria and Rosmarie had taken three days off work, to spend the time up there with the deer together.

Rosmarie was very excited. She was looking forward to spending the weekend together with her mother and her grandmother. This would be a first: she could not remember having ever spent a weekend just with her mother and her grandmother before. When she was a child, her mother had brought her to her grandmother often, but she had not stayed. Rosmarie thought it was not only because she was working, but also because of grandfather Viktor. Anyhow, she never had spent a weekend with her mother and her grandmother in the forest before. She still was upset that the deer had been shot, but it had brought her mother and grandmother together, and now the three of them were going to spent three days together! That was what Rosmarie had always wished and longed for: being with each other, spending time together, creating a sense of family, bonding and belonging.

The weekend was wonderful. They nursed the deer and they spent some time strolling through the forest and foraging the first herbs of the spring. Frieda started knitting a coat for the deer. Viktoria carved a wooden bowl for the deer to drink water from because it did not like to drink from the metal pot they had brought for it. Rosmarie made thick mattresses from straw and made a table from wood she had found in the forest. Whilst they worked on their handicrafts, they shared stories. Frieda and Rosmarie let Viktoria in on their secret of the fellowship of the unicorn. Viktoria was astonished. She had not known about their ancestresses being guardians. But most of all she was baffled that Frieda was a guardian secretly.

The three of them had not spent this much time together in years. Rosmarie could not remember having had so much time with mum and grandma since she was a little child. She enjoyed it very much and her mother and grandmother seemed to enjoy it too. They sat in the straw near the deer, drinking herbal tea, and telling each other stories of the ancestresses, the witches, and the unicorns. Rosmarie felt that through the time together and all the storytelling, she got to know her mother and her grandmother. There was so much she had not known about them.

ENCHANTMENT

They had spent the night at the farm of an elderly couple. They were old friends of grandmother Annemarie. They had spent the evening talking and they were very fascinated to hear about her journey. They said it was a wonderful story and they encouraged her to write a book about it. Mary Rose said, she might do that one day, but first she needed to find out how the story would go. She left the farm at dawn and met several herds of deer as they rode across the fields. Travelling by horse was something special. It was unique. The experience was intense. One was as close to nature as it was possible to be. Even when out walking, one wasn't as close to nature, nor as much part of it, as when riding a horse. That was what Mary Rose realised when they set off on their ride that morning. If Mary Rose had been walking the deer probably would have run away at first sight. But as she was on the horse, they watched and observed them but did not run away unless

Mary Rose and the horse came really close. The deer recognised that the horse was not a predator. Probably its smell covered hers so they thought there was just a horse. And after all Mary Rose was not a predator either, being a vegetarian all her life. So maybe the deer simply smelled two herbivores going for a walk, not predators on the prowl.

The path led through a field along a forest. At one point the field ended and the forest lined the path on both sides. The trees were taller and thicker the further they rode into the forest. The trunks of some old oaks were easily two meters thick. The forest was deep green and misty. Rays of sunlight shone through the canopy and threw a spotlight on the forest floor. Dew drops sparkled in the sunlight. A stream burbled along and filled the forest hall with a gentle melody. Birds sang along to it. The rhythmic clatter of the hooves gave the music a beat. The air smelled humid and fresh, woody and mossy. It smelled of the clear water of the stream and the fresh morning air. It smelled of the steaming mist that rose in the sunlight from the grass, the flowers and the trees. It smelled of soil.

Mary Rose took a deep breath. She closed her eyes and lifted her arms towards the sunlight as the horse walked under a break in the canopy. She saw the crowns of the trees above her. She saw the sky. She felt the rhythmic walk of the horse. She felt the freshness of the air in the forest. She felt how it revitalised her. She heard the music of the forest, the sound of the stream, the song of the birds. She felt, that she was part of nature, part of the Earth. She felt that she was alive and she sensed what a gift that was. It was a present, a wonder.

'Magic,' she thought, 'is inherent to life. Life itself is magic. And all that lives is miraculous. We should cherish life. And we should care for everything that is alive.'

This was the thought she was having when she realised that she was riding through a wonderful forest on the back of a magic horse. For the rest of the day Mary Rose remained amazed. She let the horse carry her through magic forests. She listened to the burbling streams, the singing birds. She admired the huge, ancient trees. She wondered how many decades they had stood there, and what they had witnessed. She saw squirrels, rabbits and deer. She noticed that the animals - just like the people in the town - stopped and watched her and her horse walking along the forest path on their long journey to the mountains.

"Maybe the animals are enchanted too by our appearance? Just like the people, they are suddenly reminded that once there was a time when magic horses roamed the forests. Maybe they have been waiting for the return of the unicorn that fills the air with light!"

The horse snorted and nodded with its head. Mary Rose had once taught it to do this as a trick for a show at a local horse fair. But the horse had been doing it by itself ever since when asked a question.

Mary Rose smiled. "Yes, you are a magic horse. You have even learned to speak to humans that have forgotten to speak and listen with their heart and need obvious shakes of the head to understand."

The horse snorted again.

At some point she stopped and took the saddle off the horse. She wanted to inhale the atmosphere of the forest. She sat down on a tree-trunk and did nothing but opening all her senses for the beauty of the forest. After a while she took her mobile phone and took some pictures of the horse in the beautiful forest and some selfies of herself and the horse. She sent the pictures to her grandmother, her parents and her uncle. Then she took her diary and started writing.

Maybe that is my purpose? Maybe I am an interpreter. I can understand horses, how they sense, how they are. I can make horses understand what humans want from them. Maybe I can also make humans understand what horses want? If only I could find words for all the bliss that horses bring to me. If only I could find words to describe my experiences - the connectedness; the sense of freedom and belonging; the calming and healing moments with a grazing horse; the touching experience when it gently blows in your face to say hello; the joy of flying on the back of a galloping horse; the feeling of eternal freedom on a ride through the wide open land; the enchantment of riding through a forest and seeing the deer watching us; the strength, the power, the spirit of life, the will to live, to always go forward and never give up. I am eternally grateful for all the bliss the horses brought to my life. I often ask myself how could I give something back and what could I do for them? Maybe the answer is to try to make humans understand horses. If humans appreciated horses more, horses would not be doomed to live in narrow boxes, be exploited so much, nor slaughtered for their flesh. I must take responsibility and find a way to explain to people the magic of horses. But even if I could find the right words, people who have never loved a horse may not be able to understand it. People who never loved a horse are oblivious. How could I

wake those people up? How could I possibly explain to people,
who do not love horses, and do not think that animals have
consciousness, that horses can take you to a magical world?

Mary Rose liked that thought. She let it settle for a while. Then she lay down in the grass and took a quick nap before the she continued her ride. They still had some distance to make to reach their quarters before it got dark.

The coming days they managed to make their daily distance and reach their quarters day after day. They met lovely people on their way. All of their hosts were very welcoming, hospitable, and generous. A lot of the people she met were amazed and inspired by Mary Rose and the horse, by their mission and their partnership. In turn, they were an inspiration for Mary Rose. She grew more and more confident. She should have started a blog she thought, she would have many followers by now. And that was what she did. She created a blog and put some of the pictures on there and wrote a view lines about her mission. Another couple who hosted her and her horse for a night said, she should write a book about her mission and bring together her story and her grandmother's story. Mary Rose started to think that it actually was a good idea. She would write in her diary every day and upon her return, she might turn it into a book. Yet, even though she grew more confident, she still wondered how the story would end.

LEGACY

Under a full moon, Rosmarie heard the great hart sigh deeply. Then she saw a shooting star. Her heart stopped beating for a moment. She looked over to the deer. She got up quietly and went over to it. It did not move. It had sighed out its last breath. Rosmarie kneeled down and prayed for the spirit of the deer. Whatever was to come after death, she hoped the great hart would be safe. She hoped it would not have to suffer anymore. She remembered that her grandmother Maria Rosa once told her that when a living being dies, a light goes out on Earth. But a moment later, a star lit up in the sky. She liked to believe what her grandmother told her. It was a soothing story and it gave her hope in this hour of death. She looked up to the skies and cried freely.

It was some time before her hands stopped shivering. Eventually she managed to type a message to her mother and her grandmother: "A great spirit transcended in this full moon night. A light went out on Earth. A star was lit in the sky."

Their replies came almost instantly. She was glad to read the same message from both of them: 'Will be there as soon as possible'.

People who knew that the only right thing to do, if death came and took a loved one away, was to be there - those were the people who understood and truly cared. Rosmarie was crying as she waited for them. She did not have to wait long; both arrived quickly in spite of the journey they had to make. Viktoria checked the deer and nodded solemnly. A tear ran across her cheek. They fell into each others's arm and held each other tightly.

Frieda, Viktoria and Rosmarie wept together. They shed many tears. They felt the same pain. Viktoria's whole body was shaking. She had cramps and the tears streamed across her cheeks. Frieda and Rosmarie held her tight in their arms. The pain kept shaking her and she could hardly breathe. Rosmarie felt helpless. There was nothing she could do. The deer was dead. The only thing they could do for Viktoria was to be there and go with her through the pain. After a while, Frieda started humming a melody. Rosmarie knew the melody, because her grandmother used to sing it to her when she was a child. It was a lullaby. It helped. Viktoria stopped shivering. She was so weak that she just lay in Frieda's arms. Together Rosmarie and Frieda helped her to the straw bed in the cocoon. They sat down on both sides of her and covered her in thick blankets. Then she calmed down a little. Frieda whispered:

"Losing one's spirit animal is an extremely painful thing. You feel the pain in your body when it dies, and you think you have lost it, as it leaves this Earth and heads off to other dimensions. You will feel this pain for a while. And you will feel weak. That is because you lose your strength when your spirit animal dies. You will go through the gloomy valley of mourning. There you will encounter hatred and anger, pain and despair, doubt, guilt and hopelessness. Be aware of the dangers of the valley of mourning, keep going even when you are exhausted and do not fall victim to one of these feelings. But then, if you succeed and keep going, you will one day leave the valley of mourning. For some it takes only a few month; for some a year; for some it takes many years. There are also those who never find a way out again, but remain caught in there for the rest of their lives."

Frieda paused for a moment and looked at Viktoria and Rosmarie. They nodded sadly. They both thought of Viktor.

Then Frieda continued to speak: "Remember to be brave. Keep going. Life lives on. Love loves on. Light shines on. Those things are connected and connect us all. One life ceases, another life is born. As long as you live love truly and shine light wherever you are. When you finally succeed in leaving the valley of mourning, the wounds will stop bleeding. Scars will remain. The good memories will come back. Then the light will start to shine once again in your heart. When you realise that you can never truly lose your spirit animal as it is a part of you, then you will gain strength and you will rise up even stronger than you were before. When you realise you will love your spirit animal forever, then you will know that love is more than a partnership of two creatures; it is bigger, it is all-encompassing, it is life."

Her words were powerful and impressive even though Frieda had only whispered them. Silence fell for some time. Finally Viktoria nodded and said:

"Thank you. I know. I saw you rise again after you lost yours."

"Thank you my beloved daughter. That indeed makes me proud," Frieda replied.

"What was your spirit animal?" Rosmarie wanted to know.

"It was a cow."

"Herta? The best cow you ever had?"

"Yes, my darling, Herta."

Rosmarie had not felt that close to her mother and her grandmother ever since she had been a child.

"Will I have a spirit animal too? How will I know that it is my spirit animal?" Rosmarie asked her grandmother.

"Yes, you will have one too. You just know."

Rosmarie nodded.

"Sometimes, if you are lucky, you may even have more than one. I am sure that Rolf is also my spirit animal. He is very different from the first one, but he complements it somehow. Maybe it is because I have changed so much? Or maybe I have changed so much because of the new spirit animal? Anyhow, you can have more than one spirit animal in your life."

"Grandma, can you tell us the story of the red stag you used to tell me when I was a child?"

"Alright," Frieda said, and she cleared her throat and put on her story-telling voice. "When the last unicorn left this valley, it chose a successor. It was a hind whose fur was orange-red like the sunset. Just like many of the great spirits and magical creatures, it was hunted by a greedy man who wanted to own the hind. He tried to shoot it because he wanted to stuff it and hang it up on the wall of his living room. When will humans understand that you cannot possess the light of another living being? When will they learn that one cannot be enriched by taking the life of another creature? His heart was hardened, and he did not understand that it was his own responsibility to hold a light of love in his heart. He was ignorant, cruel and greedy. When he saw the red deer, he was not enlightened by its appearance. Instead he wanted to own it, to have its light, to capture its magic, and so he shot it. The hind was mortally wounded but it escaped. It hid somewhere in the mountain forest and gave birth to a calf before it died. A light went out on Earth, but a new life was born. The young deer would have died as well, if not for a young girl who spent the summer in the mountains herding her father's goats. The goats led her through the thickest forest on the steepest hill, up towards the rock wall that reached hundreds of meters up into the sky. There she found the baby deer. One of her goats adopted the deer, and they spent the summer up in the mountains together. The deer grew quickly and it became big and strong. Soon, it could live on its own and it often left the goat herd to roam the forests. When autumn came, the girl had to say goodbye to the deer. She still was young but she had become a guardian. The baby deer had become a big stag and a great spirit. They were connected for life - and beyond - as the stag was her spirit animal. He grew to be an impressive great hart and guarded over the forest."

"Mum is the young girl, isn't she?"

Frieda nodded.

Viktoria smiled and kissed her mother.

"You told this story to my daughter? That is so wonderful. I cannot believe you knew it all this time."

Frieda smiled. "It is good to keep some things a secret."

Viktoria agreed. After a while she started speaking: "It is just so senseless. He grew up to be a majestic great hart, against all the odds. Then he dies like this. I know I should not let hatred grow and fester inside of me, but I really want the hunter to pay for this."

Frieda responded in a gentle and quiet voice: "Legacy," she said. "Think of its legacy. That might save you from losing your mind over the senselessness of this act and vengeful thoughts. Just consider how it has brought us together. It chose Rosmarie as a guardian just a few weeks before it died. As if it had known. Maybe it did know? Maybe it knew its time had come to transcend and wanted to leave? Why did it show itself to the hunter? The deer was so smart it could be invisible if it wanted to be. The hunter was after it for many years. He never had even really seen it. But then, that night - under a new moon - it walked right in front of the hunter's raised hide. It knew that the hunter was there. It wanted to appear to him. It led Rosmarie to the secret circle. It ran into her arms and made her call you and me. Maybe it was saying, we need to stand by each other? Maybe it wanted to bring us together. Maybe it wanted to see you again."

Viktoria sobbed deeply.

Frieda paused for a while. Then she continued speaking:

"It has chosen a successor. It has brought us together. It has united us and swore us to be the witches, guardians, and companions of the great spirits. The great hart is one of the great spirits. Just like the unicorn, it chooses its fellows. If it appears, it is a summoning. When it appears to you, when you see it in the forest, when it comes to you in your dream, you are called to become a fellow of the light, a keeper of love, a guardian of life. When the last unicorn left, the deer took the post as ambassador of light, love, and life. That is what it stands for. If it shows itself to you, if it appears, it is to call you to take responsibility, to live a life of caring and compassion. It reminds you that your purpose on Earth is to love, to preserve life, to shine your light and light it in the hearts of others. This is its legacy."

THE CENTAUR

*T*he journey along the British coast had been smooth and enjoyable. Once the first few of days had gone according to her plan Mary Rose was able to relax. From then on, it had been a wonderful trekking ride. There had been days where she just enjoyed the ride - nothing else. She still had the importance of the mission on her mind, but she was able to simply enjoy the journey. After all she had always wanted to go on an extended trek. And now here she was, on a cross-country ride with a goal. She couldn't have asked for more.

Now she noticed that she had left the lovely country-side behind her. By midday, they had left behind the green hills with their grazing sheep. Now there was more concrete as they entered the industrial area of the harbour town. The houses stood closer together, and they were not as neat as those, she had seen before. There were no more gardens, more rubbish, and it looked like nobody here had time or money to refurbish the buildings. There were more cars driving on the roads and it was noisy. The people she encountered looked sullenly and peered suspiciously at her.

Mary Rose did not like it at all. The horse did not like it either. She could feel that the horse was less relaxed, more tense, more alert. It had its head up, and its ears were moving fast in the directions of all the unfamiliar noises. Mary Rose was feeling the same. She was tense, alert, but she had not found another way even after looking at the maps again and again, and she even talked with the ferryman on the phone. There was no other way. Apparently, this was the only ferry that allowed horses on board. So they had to get through it somehow.

The port, where livestock was loaded on the ship, was at the outskirts of the port town in a rough industrial area. The area was poor, the houses dirty. In decades past, it had been a working class district serving the port and the ships. During the war it became a ghetto for refugees, where many people who fled from the war had arrived. Today it was a district where low income workers lived. It was gloomy, dirty, and poor.

Mary Rose noticed that the people she met here seemed indifferent to them. They looked at them distrustfully. She thought: 'Maybe people who are very poor and have to fight for their survival every day, people who worry how they will make ends meet when they wake up in the morning; maybe those people cannot sense the lightness of life in the same way as some others can, who have fewer things preying on their minds. They cannot pause and watch us. They have a burden to carry and work to make ends meet.' It made her thoughtful.

She rode towards the harbour. The lanes narrowed, and there were big warehouses to both sides. The horse grew more and more nervous. Eventually it had its head up high, the whites of the eyes showing. It was close to panicking. It kept trying to turn around and head back in the other direction. Mary Rose stopped the horse. She became acutely aware of a foetid smell. Then she saw they were near a slaughterhouse, and next to it there were barns. The lane reeked of death. That was what the horse wanted to tell her: 'it smells of death, let's go the other way!'

Mary Rose felt sick. It was somehow the worst possible situation. She could not ask her horse to go that way, could she? It knew already that there was a slaughterhouse. The slaughterhouse was right next to the harbour, and beside it there was a barn. Was this the barn where the ferryman had said she could keep her horse for the night? Next to a slaughterhouse? How insensitive was that? She would not put her horse in that barn.

She looked into a side lane and saw two men beating a cow out of a lorry. Mary Rose could not watch it. But she could not look away either. The horse was frozen with panicked eyes. What should she do? She felt helpless. There was not much she could do. It was legal to kill animals and bring them to slaughter, but unnecessary cruelty was not. She decided that if she could not save the cow, she could maybe give those brutal men a warning. She took out her phone and filmed the scene as she fought back the tears. The realisation that there was nothing else she could really do to help this poor creature made her feel sick and powerless.

"Hey!" She shouted at them. "I've got all that on video. I will take it to the police if you don't stop!"

When the men saw her, they walked towards her quickly. For a moment, Mary Rose was unable to move. She felt frozen and unable to decide what to do. She felt helpless but the men were coming. They yelled at her and started to run towards her. One of them cursed her, called her awful names and he swung his stick in a threatening way. He shouted at her that he would do harm to her and her horse if she would not delete that video. They came closer with heavy steps.

The horse was prancing nervously. It wanted to run away. Mary Rose felt sorry for the cow, but what could she do to help it? She could not just ride away, could she? She must tell the police about the animal abuse. Would they care? Probably not, the policemen knew it was legal to kill cows. What could she do? She was still filming. The men had threatened her. That was not legal. She could use that against them. The men might have had a tough life and they had the worst work of all, but they had no right to torment animals and they had no right to threaten a young woman. There was no justification for that. Every human is responsible for their actions.

In the next second, the men reached the horse and one of them tried to catch the reins. In the same moment the horse reared and kicked out with its fore legs. Mary Rose reached around its neck to stop herself falling off. One of the horse's hooves struck the man on the shoulder and he fell to the ground. The horse had decided to fight for their lives so it had defended both, its own life and that of its human companion too. It came down for a second and reared again and the other man jumped aside to not get kicked and lay next to the other on the ground.

The horse was moving quickly, and Mary Rose felt herself instinctively moving with it, as if they were one. They became one big warrior with four legs and four hard hooves, two arms and two heads. The one creature was big, wild and threatening. In that moment Mary Rose remembered her grandfather Graham telling her:

"The greatest knights, those that were invincible, they had a secret weapon: They possessed the ability to become one with their horses. When they were one, they could lead their horses by thought transference. Well, it might have been invisible signals given by shifting the body weight. Either way, they were superior to their opponents because those who had not developed such a partnership with their horses could never rely on them in the battle because their horses were trying to escape in the first place. Legends were told about the centaur. They are half horse, half human and they were considered the strongest warriors of all."

Mary Rose just realised that for a moment she and her horse had been one, moving as one creature, they were a centaur for a few seconds. She hated the situation she was in, but at the same time it was the ultimate test. It was not a challenge Gordon made up. This was real. And she knew in that moment that her grandfather would have been proud to see how she and her horse acted as one in the fight.

The men were lying on the ground, now terrified. They knew this horse could kill them easily with its hoofs. Mary Rose knew that these men had wanted to harm her, and she did not even want to think about what they were capable of doing to her horse if they had free hand and they realised they could not break its spirit. A feeling of hatred and abhorrence rose inside her. The feeling was strong. She detested these men so much. Now they were lying there in the dirt. She remained motionless and stared at them. She had to summon all her self-control to not let her feelings of anger and hatred take over.

What followed was a battle. A battle that Mary Rose fought inside of her. Her feelings of hatred were so strong, they were about to take over. She could feel that there was a force inside her that wanted to take revenge and punish those men that were cruel to helpless creatures and freely threatened those of whom they thought were weaker than themselves. Had those who did not respect the lives of others deserve respect for theirs? The feelings of hatred and disgust were about to take control of her. In the same moment the horse reared again and it was about to attack the men. She sensed how it tensed its forelegs. She knew that it would hit the ground with its hoofs and with full power. Mary Rose knew that this could kill the men.

In mid-air it felt like everything was happening in slow motion suddenly. The horse was coming down and it was a fraction of a second before its hoofs would hit the ground. There was a feeling getting through to Mary Rose that asked for mercy. In the same moment she regained full consciousness, she breathed out and let go of the hatred. Instantly she felt pity for the men. In the same second the horse hit the ground with its hoofs with a massive stamp. It was silent for a moment and nothing moved. The horse's hoofs had just missed the men. They were pale and scared to death. The horse snorted into their panicking face. It had spared their lives.

Mary Rose was very impressed by what just had happened. Was it true? A knight could guide her horse with thoughts. And when human and horse were one, they could communicate with thoughts and feelings? Amazing, wasn't it? It was an overwhelming feeling. She looked at the men and spoke:

"You are lucky. The horse has mercy for you. Even though I am not sure you even deserve it. Remember that."

She turned around and the horse started off in a gallop. The hoofs were like thunder on the ground. It wanted to get away from these men. At the next corner she asked her horse to stop. The horse was in no mood to obey; it wanted to run away from them. But it stopped reluctantly, hopping and bucking in protest against Mary Rose's decision. She needed a moment to get her mind focused again and then she decided to look for the police. She searched on her phone for the police station and rode towards it.

She was overwhelmed by a storm of emotions. Her heart was bumping, adrenalin had kicked in. She still felt the pain of seeing the brutal reality of what humans do to animals. She felt helpless and powerless. She felt the anger and hatred against these men, and yet she knew they were only puppets in the machinery of the meat industry. She felt upset about the realisation how fast evil feelings took control of her. She was glad that she could regain the power and avert her harmful thoughts.

She was amazed about the feeling of being one with her horse. And whilst she had always believed that the horse could read her thoughts and sense her feelings, she realised in this moment that she could also sense the horse's feelings.

Mary Rose stroke the neck of her horse and said to it in thought:

"We were one. Our connection was so close, we could sense each others thoughts and feelings. We were a centaur. Half human, half horse."

The horse snorted and nodded with its head. Mary Rose laughed out loud. She was relieved.

After a few minutes she found the police office. She told the police what had happened, and they drove off to look for the men. In the meantime she had to make a statement and she allowed the police to take a copy of her video as evidence. It took some time and by the time she left the police office it was already getting dark.

'Oh no!' Mary Rose was getting worried. Dusk was falling and she had no place to stay for the night. She felt drained. She was hungry and so was the horse. She had no idea where to go now. This was the first night that had not gone to plan, and it was the worst place to be in. In the forest, maybe, she would have dared to sleep outside. The horse would have found some grass. But here? In the roughest district of the industrial port town, there was nowhere to go. How would she feed her horse? She stood underneath a street lamp and stared at her map.

LIFE

*S*pring had made the forest bloom into a paradise. The world woke from its winter sleep and new life sprouted everywhere. The days were long, sunny and warm. Leaves and flowers grew silently. Birds sang. Bees buzzed. Trees had new shoots and the plants of the forest sprang up. New life was born. Everything was changing. The forest was full of flowers and presented itself in the brightest green. The highland plain turned into a fruitful and friendly valley.

Rosmarie walked through the enchanted forest. It was wonderful. If one left the path where all the people walked, and took the small and narrow path that led straight up into the depths of the forest, one could watch the life of the forest taking place. There was a fir tree that was a home to a clan of blue tits. Rosmarie stood still and leaned against a tree. She watched the bird family following their everyday life in the tree. It made her smile. Somehow it made her happy. She was not sure why, but it made her heart feel light and filled with love - or maybe life? It was just life itself - in all its facets and its richness - that fascinated Rosmarie every time anew. It was life that was so miraculous. Those tiny little birds that lived up here were wonderful. They were amazing. How could they survive the winters up here in the mountains? They were beautiful. Their blue and yellow feathers were nothing less than marvellous. How they lived together in this big tree, with its dense branches and thick needles was just amazing. Their singing was melodious and filled the forest with an ode to life. How could that not make her happy?

Rosmarie continued her stroll through the forest. She saw a hare. It hopped across the woodland and ate from the fresh sprouts of the spring forest. It had been a long and harsh winter, and the animal needed the power of the young shoots to revitalise. It was amazing, Rosmarie thought, how the world changed, how the highland valley turned from a frozen, icy, crystalline winter wonderland into a blossoming, fruitful meadow and a forest, growing food for the hare, the deer, and all the other animals living up here.

After a while she came to a forest clearing. The sun's rays broke through the young and pale green leaves and shone a golden light on the grassland. Rosmarie felt how the beauty of the light and the vitality of the sprouting spring forest filled her with a bright, warm energy.

She walked to the middle of the clearing, where the sun's rays shone through a break in the trees, creating a spotlight like the arena of a circus. She stopped in the full glow of the sun's rays and stretched with her hands up towards the sky. She took off her shoes and stood there, barefoot. She imagined herself as a tree, rooted to the ground, to the Earth, with her branches reaching towards the sky and the sunlight. She enjoyed being a tree. It gave her strength. It recharged her with energy. Energy that she would need to pass her final exams, and more: she often thought about which path she should choose afterwards. She felt torn between her beloved highland valley, where she felt rooted, and the desire to study law and take an influential position in society. She loved being up here, but she did not want to be a waitress her entire life. She needed to explore other options. She could move to the town and study there, and return as often as possible to the highland valley. And the horse? Could she afford it while she studied? How could she manage all of this? Study, earn money, become influential in society, be a guardian of the highland valley, bring her family together, adopt a horse, and maybe one day, she would want to find a partner and have a family on top of that. Well, that was an ambitious list!

Rosmarie was still standing in the clearing like a human tree. She tried not to worry. 'I will find my path. I have to trust in my abilities and I have to find the courage to follow my heart. I must find the strength to make all my dreams come true,' she thought. She took a deep breath. She closed her eyes and breathed the fresh air of the spring forest. She felt the sun rays on her face. She smiled. 'Yes, I will find my way,' she said to herself in thoughts.

She opened her eyes again and she saw them: a group of red deer wandering along the edges of the forest. There were several females, and three of them had fawns: two brownish-red ones and one fiery-red one. Rosmarie smiled. Life was fantastic, wasn't it?

The fresh air of the spring revived Rosmarie, and she felt like walking and climbing a peak, which had been covered by snow for months. She hiked upwards towards the peak. After an hour's walk she spotted something moving amongst the grey boulders. She stopped. She watched for a short while and saw a group of three chamois. She smiled and continued walking. Finally she reached the peak and sat down to take a rest. But she was not the only one drawn to the top of the peak. There were others too, who wanted to enjoy this view over the awakening valley, now that the peak was finally clear of snow. At first she saw an ibex, that set off with massive leaps across the rocks and boulders when it spotted her. Then she saw a person mounting the steep path. Somebody she recognised.

Rosmarie's emotions flared. She felt anger, hatred, pity, and at the same time she called upon herself for forgiveness. What should she say? How should she react? She had hot and cold flushes, she thought about telling him that she knew, she thought about pretending she did not know anything. Her grandmother had asked her to not say anything, lest they reveal their secret. But at the same time, she did not want to let him get away with it. She needed to do something. But what? She could not decide on a solution since her emotions were too confusing. She came to no conclusion, and soon enough she ran out of time. The huntsman stood in front of her.

"Good morning," he said.

Rosmarie grumbled something.

The huntsman opened his bag. He took a bundle out

of it. It was moving. He took a blanket off to reveal a young eagle. Without her asking for an explanation he started to tell her: "I found it in autumn. I took it home and raised it. Now it is time to set it free."

Rosmarie was astonished. "You are not going to kill it, stuff it and hang it up on your wall?" She just could not resist asking him.

The huntsman gave her a long and examining look. "No," he finally answered. "I have decided to set it free. I admit this was not my original intention. But I changed my mind. I have decided it is time to do things differently."

"Wow, I am truly amazed. How come?"

"Well, let's say, I had a spiritual experience. I was - it sounds a bit far-fetched, but I think I was enlightened."

"Oh that is wonderful. Would you share your experience with me?"

"Umm," he was hesitant. "Let's say, I had a vision."

"A vision? Really? What was it? Don't tell me you saw the unicorn! I have been waiting all my life for it to appear!"

The huntsman looked at her with obvious surprise in his face. After a while he replied: "No, not a unicorn. A great hart appeared to me."

"Oh, really? I am a bit jealous I must say."

The huntsman smiled nervously. "Yes, I am lucky. It changed me. It made me want to change my life. I now want to protect life. I have been talking to the mayor about creating a wildlife reserve up here."

Now Rosmarie was really astonished. "What a wonderful idea! I'd be more than willing to support you, and help make your vision come true," she replied straight away.

The huntsman gave her a long thoughtful look. Then he proffered his hand. They shook. "Deal. I could indeed use your help. You could start talking to your grandfathers and the landlord of the alpine hut, and lobby for the project."

"I will."

Then they let the eagle fly into the sky. They watched it fly over the highland valley in big circles. The eagle was soaring.

THE UNICORN RIDER

*M*ary Rose just wanted to get away from this miserable place. She decided to ride to the edge of the suburbs. On her map it looked like there was something greenish along the train tracks on the far side. Maybe she could find some grass there? She would not sleep tonight. She would not be able to close her eyes in this unwelcoming area. She would stay awake and guard the horse. She started heading in that direction.

She was still upset about the events at the harbour. She hated that people killed animals and there was nothing she could do about it. It was legal. Mary Rose thought of the stories of the unicorns. Legends told that once there were magic horses living in the forests all over Europe. But people hunted them for the magical properties of their blood and their horn. They hunted them until not one was left. That was how some humans behaved, they were greedy, cruel, selfish and ignorant. Unfortunately, these people often managed to get into powerful positions of society.

'Perhaps,' Mary Rose thought, 'I should do what my parents want me to do: I should study law and then I could use it to help those who need it and bring wrong-doers to justice. Eventually that would help the animals more than being a trainer.'

Mary Rose was shattered. Was this the end of her journey? Would it end here? Had she failed to complete the mission, or was this its purpose all along? To realise that violence was stronger than life, that love could not heal evil, that she needed to study law and become powerful in society to protect life and change some-thing? Was that the message? Were her parents right after all? She slumped listlessly in her saddle, close to tears. Mary Rose felt lost. She did not know how to go on, so she let the horse take the lead.

On the outskirts of the suburbs besides the train-tracks the horse found some grass and ate leafs of a bush. Mary Rose got off the horse and looked around for a while. When nothing moved in the dark, she relaxed a little bit and sat down close besides the horse. She was preparing for a night outside. She did not feel comfort-able. She was scared. It got darker and darker, until she herself could not see anything in the dark. She could only rely on her horse's ears and eyes. She followed her horse step by step. She did not close one eye that night. The night felt endless, cold and dark. Luckily it did not rain and the wind was not harsh. Nevertheless Mary Rose felt chilly and she was exhausted. When dawn was finally breaking, she was relieved that the night was over. Still, she had no plan what do. She rode further out of the town towards a green space she could see in some distance. When they reached the field she let the horse have its breakfast.

Mary Rose was hungry, cold and tired. And what was worst, she just had lost all hope that she could complete her journey. She was shattered. In this moment she heard the sound of fluttering wings. She looked up as a sparrow flew over her head. It landed on a street lamp and looked at her. After a moment it started flying again. It flew a loop over the horse and then flew away across the field. The horse started trotting in the direction the sparrow had flown. It seemed it wanted to run with the sparrow. When Mary Rose whistled it waited for her. She got on the horse and it fell into a trot. Then it ran faster, building up to a canter to keep up with the sparrow.

The sparrow landed a wooden, seemingly hand-made street sign. In big colourful letters it was saying: Animal shelter. Mary Rose gave the sparrow a nod and she rode along the uneven, unpaved path in the direction the sign pointed. After a ten minutes ride she saw a small farmstead in the distance. It was a tiny house made from grey bricks surrounded by pastures and she could see all sorts of animals strolling around. There were horses, donkeys, cows, pigs, sheep, goats, chicken and geese. Mary Rose felt relieved. Hopefully she could get hay for her horse there!

The animals paused and looked at her and her horse as they came down the path. Then the door of the old dilapidated shed opened and an elderly lady stepped out. Her hair was grey and her skin was tanned by wind and sun. She was pushing a wheelbarrow that she put down as she saw the horse and Mary Rose. She rubbed her hands on the pair of dungarees. The lady looked at her and smiled. She had a warm and generous expression in her face. She came towards Mary Rose and she said in a warm voice: "Welcome! Be my guest."

Mary Rose was so glad to meet a warm and friendly person in this area. The lady treated her like an old friend whom she had been expecting. Mary Rose dismounted while the lady admired the horse. She reached a hand carefully towards it. The horse responded by touching her hand with its nose and allowing her to stroke its neck. Mary Rose was relieved. The horse's ability to judge a person's character was infallible. She took the offer very gratefully. The lady led them to a shed next to the house where a flock of sheep, a donkey and a pony lived. It was dry and there was hay and water. The horse seemed to be comfortable. Then Mary Rose followed the lady to the house and sat down in the living room, where she was served a cup of tea, soup and toast. Mary Rose told her that she wanted to cross the channel but the livestock ferry was full of slaughter animals. She told the woman of her horror at the suffering of the animals and about being terrified by the men who worked there.

"Don't worry. I will get you across. There is another way. If the horse is in a trailer it can be on the car-ferry. But first you should get some rest. You are exhausted. Eat your soup and then take a nap. After you rested, we will arrange everything."

Mary Rose nodded gratefully. She took a nap at the woman's house. She fell asleep straight away, even though it was early in the morning. When she woke up it was midday. She got dressed and walked downstairs. Nobody was there so she went outside to the shed. As she entered the shed silently, she saw a young woman sitting on a bale of straw admiring her horse. She even talked to it:

"You are an extraordinary beautiful horse. Do you know that?"

The horse snorted and nodded. Mary Rose grinned, she loved how her horse learned to do this and to baffle people all the time. It worked. The young woman was surprised and looked at the horse unbelievingly. Then she said breathless:

"You are a special horse, you understand every word. Are you a unicorn?"

The horse snorted and nodded again. Mary Rose held her hand over her mouth to prevent herself from laughing out loud. This horse was just too brilliant.

"You know, my grandmother used to tell me a story of a unicorn that lived in the forest of my homeland. That is far away, east from here. My grandma said the unicorn can read human's minds and hearts."

Then the young woman got up and approached the horse slowly. It allowed her to touch it and she started stroking its shoulder and its back.

Mary Rose sneaked a few steps back out and then came in again with more heavy steps. Now the woman heard her coming. She looked at Mary Rose with her intense yellowish-brown eyes.

"Hello. I see my horse made a new friend. I am Mary Rose." Mary Rose held out her hand.

The woman shook her hand and said: "Pleasure, Tsura."

Mary Rose noticed that Tsura gave her a long scanning look, but she could not quite tell why. Was she jealous because she had such a beautiful horse?

Tsura then took the shovel and continued to muck out the stables. Mary Rose took a shovel as well and helped her. Whilst they were working side by side, Tsura wanted to know where she came from and where she was heading to. Mary Rose told her the story of her grandmother and since she had already heard that Tsura had had a unicorns-inspired childhood as well and she had the suspicion that she would understand what her and her grandmother were talking about, she told Tsura:

"It is my grandmother's last wish. She asked me to return the fortune of the unicorn to the woman who once gave it to her. That's how she calls it."

Tsura looked at her with amazement in her eyes. Then she stammered to the great surprise of Mary Rose:

"Unicorn Rider."

'A woman who recognises my true self,' Mary Rose thought to herself. She smiled. She was flattered by the young woman's words. She liked to be called the Unicorn Rider.

Tsura was curious to know how it happened that Mary Rose came to this remote shelter. Mary Rose explained her situation, and that she felt, she just could not load her horse onto a ship full of slaughter animals. It would be awful for both of them. And she felt so helpless that she could not help the suffering animals. This all came out in a flood as, for some reason, she felt that she could confide in this woman.

Tsura looked at Mary Rose silently. Then she responded: "You are compassionate. You can sense their fear, their pain, but also their bliss. You are a special human being. That is why, you were chosen."

Mary Rose was flattered, even though she did not quite understand what Tsura meant. "Chosen?" She repeated the words and tried to capture their meaning.

Tsura looked at her for a while without saying anything. It was as if she was waiting for her words to settle.

Mary Rose was lost in thought for a moment. 'Chosen for what? Chosen by whom?' She looked at Tsura again and asked: "What do you mean?"

Tsura let her wait for a while longer. It was as if she was waiting for Mary Rose to find the answer herself. Eventually she added:

"Unicorns choose their rider. It is not the other way around."

Mary Rose wanted to add something when they heard the sound of engines. Tsura went outside to see who was coming. Mary Rose followed her. It was Lady Sally, as Tsura called the landlady who owned the shelter. She drove along the uneven path with an old jeep and a horse-trailer. She stopped in the courtyard and turned the car and drove backwards towards the round-pen. When she got out of the car she waved the young women over. They came closer as she as she opened the ramp. Lady Sally said:

"Now look at this beautiful horse. It used to be a show-jumper but now it refuses to jump. So they sent it to slaughter. The man in the slaughterhouse called me. He said its is completely healthy and in good shape. He said he would not want to kill it. So I went to pick it up. And here it is!"

Lady Sally unloaded the horse into the round pen. It was very hectic, it whinnied and snorted and ran in circles. Lady Sally looked at Mary Rose and Tsura and said: "Alright. You two get started. It would be great if you could heal the horse and I could sell it as a riding horse again. I really need money urgently to feed all the animals here."

Mary Rose looked at Tsura and said: "May I?"

Tsura nodded and Mary Rose stepped into the roundpen. The horse snorted suspiciously and ran even faster circles. It had its head up high, its eyes wide open looking over the fence and it was whinnying. Mary Rose stood in the middle and did not move. After a while the horse got calmer and slowed down and finally it dropped into a trot. It trotted in circles for a while and it stopped whinnying. Mary Rose was focused but relaxed. Then the horse turned its inside eye and ear to Mary Rose. She knew the horse was now seeking contact. She knew it might just happen in the next second that it decided to communicate with her. She must not miss the decisive moment. Mary Rose was very concentrated, but she stayed relaxed at the same time. She hoped that it might happen. She opened her heart and in her thoughts she invited the horse to connect with her. She tried to transmit a feeling of trust and respect. In that moment the horse turned its head and looked at her with both eyes. Mary Rose reacted in the same moment, she bowed gently, stepped half a step back and turned sideways to not look at the horse frontally. Then she waited motionless. The horse slowed down, turned, and walked towards her. It stopped right behind her. For a few seconds both of them remained motionless. Then Mary Rose exhaled and relaxed visibly. The horse snorted and relaxed a little bit as well. After a short while of relaxation Mary Rose started to walk. The horse followed.

Lady Sally clapped her hands. "Well done! Great job!"

Tsura smiled. When Mary Rose walked by she whispered: "Unicorn rider."

Mary Rose was happy that connecting with the horse went so smoothly. She actually would have expected the horse to run off several times because it seemed extremely stressed. But she was glad it worked at the first go. That meant this horse had good chances to be trained and find a home with a leisure riding person. The horse was better and easier than she thought. It stopped when she stopped and it followed when she walked. Probably it was glad to find a person who could communicate with it after its odyssey that seemed to end in the slaughterhouse. Then she told Tsura to take her place in the roundpen and she stood at the fence and guided Tsura. Tsura had a clear body language and a honest attitude, and soon enough the horse followed her as well. Then they started stroking the horse everywhere and they noticed it did not like being touched in the face and at the ears, it also had problems giving its hind legs. These were typical issues of horses that were lacking trust to humans. Mary Rose told Tsura to practice touching the horse until it allowed it. Tsura nodded. Mary Rose spent the whole day teaching Tsura and Lady Sally horsemanship with their various horses.

At the end of the day they sat at the dinner table. Everybody was tired but happy. Lady Sally said:

"It was good that you came. Thank you for teaching us horsemanship. You have a gift."

Mary Rose thanked her gratefully.

"But now lets go to bed. We have to catch a ferry tomorrow morning."

THE GREAT SPIRITS

*T*he coming day, Rosmarie went to see her grandmother Maria Rosa and her grandfather Erhard. She had promised to spread the word about the wildlife reserve, plus she had not visited her grandparents in a while. They lived a reclusive life in a remote part of the mountains. It required some travelling to visit them. Down at the ravine, there was a crossing. One road led up to the highland valley, and to the alpine hut. The other way was a steep path, which wound upwards through the forest to another peak. This mountain was covered by dense forests, which grew on steep slopes. The road was narrow, and led along a slope with an abyss. The forest was thick, old and wild here. It was primeval and almost untouched. In just a few places, the dense woodland opened up a little bit, and allowed space for a clearing and a meadow. This mountain was almost uninhabited by humans and its dense forests provided a refuge for animals. On this mountain, there was just one cabin. Rosmarie's grandparents were the only people living up here.

Rosmarie imagined how her father had to walk this steep road every day when he was young, and went to school down in the valley. These days, some hikers would regard his daily route down to school as a stiff workout. Her father used to walk this every day, in all weather, winter and summer, ice and heat. Her parents went to school together. It was a forbidden love story. Two families - two grandfathers, at least - who were feuding, while their children fell in love with each other. Rosmarie thought it was quite romantic, but at the same time it made their life very complicated. She had always wished for a normal family with family members being able to talk to each other. But she had given up hope that this would ever happen. It would require a miracle.

At the fork in the road, she left the main road and took the narrow path that wound up to her grandparents cabin. She did not want to have such worrisome thoughts but she could not help asking herself how they would manage if grandfather Erhard one day could not care for grandmother Maria Rosa anymore. She shook her head and tried to shake off this thought. She could worry about that when the time came. She always worried about things in the future. There was no point worrying about things that had not happened.

She was sweaty and out of breath when she arrived at her grandparents' house. The view from here was amazing. The cabin was right up by the steep mountainside. From here, one could see over the valley and to the mountains on the other side. It was beautiful. She stood still and watched the scenery with great admiration.

Grandfather's poodle had noticed her already, and it trotted towards her. Her grandfather's family had always kept poodles. They used to be hunters. Grandfather Erhard used to be a hunter himself. But one day he stopped hunting, and became a subsistence farmer, a forester, a nurse and a houseman. He cared for everything: grandmother, the animals, the house, the garden and the forest.

"A rare visitor!" Rosmarie heard a voice, and then she spotted grandfather Erhard beside the shed amidst the goat, the cow, the donkey and the chicken.

"Hi grandpa!" Rosmarie gave her grandfather a long hug. She was surprised every time by how well and how vivacious he still looked. She helped him feed the animals, and afterwards they went back to the house. Grandmother Maria Rosa was sitting in her wheelchair in front of the house, knitting. "Grandma!" Rosmarie ran towards her.

Grandmother Maria Rosa looked up and her face lit up. "My darling! Here you are!" They hugged each other.

Then Rosmarie pushed grandmother's wheelchair inside the house. Grandfather Erhard had prepared a pot of herbal tea. He put a jar of honey from his own bees on the table. He also put out homemade bread, butter and cheese, as well as eggs, pickled vegetables, and homemade herbal pesto on the table. Rosmarie felt at home straight away. She used to come here often as a child. She had always loved being with her grandparents - all four of them - but when she grew up, and she started to understand the unresolved tensions in the family, Rosmarie started to resent them. In particular, she was unhappy with Viktor and Erhard, still mired in their feud. In her teens, she had not visited her grandparents often. But now, something had changed. Perhaps she had changed?

She enjoyed being with Erhard and Maria Rosa. She told them what had happened yesterday, that she had met the huntsman and that he wanted to create a wildlife reserve in the highland valley.

"I'll believe that when I see it," Erhard muttered. "He is a man of big words, not a man of action. If he wants it, there must be something in it for him, otherwise he would not do it. He can only ever think about his profits. He cares for nothing but money, trophies and status symbols. He does not care about nature and wildlife."

"He was enlightened. He said it changed him. He wants to do things differently," Rosmarie explained, while she took a big bite from her bread with pickled cucumber, cress, mustard and horseradish.

"How? How did that happen?" Maria Rosa was curious to know.

Rosmarie noticed how she went from looking tired, to curious and interested. The fog in front of her eyes seemed to disappear, and all of a sudden her mind was clear and sharp. Those moments were rare, unfortunately. Those moments were precious. Rosmarie sensed the brightness of this moment.

"He said he had seen an apparition. A great hart appeared to him. The encounter changed him," Rosmarie continued. In secret, she was thinking about the question, whether or not the deer had known. She asked herself if the stag had been willing to make the sacrifice it required to change the huntsman, if he had been willing to give his life to change one man.

"That is wonderful!" Maria Rosa said.

"As I say, I'll believe it when I see it. He is not the kind of man that changes just like that. He must have a financial interest. There must be some profit in this for him," Erhard insisted.

"That is interesting indeed. This has happened before. There are sagas about the great spirits of the mountain forests. They rarely appear to humans. They come in different forms and shapes: horses, deer, wolves, eagles, hares, bears, sometimes as a butterfly, a bat or even a frog or fish. Often, it is a tree or a flower. The great spirits take many forms. But up here, the most legendary are the unicorn and the great hart. Both of them appear in sagas and on coats of arms and are deeply connected to the historical consciousness of people in the area. People believe that the appearance of a great spirit to a human is a sign, a message, an omen. If a great spirit appears to you, it is a calling. It is no coincidence. The great spirits remain invisible unless they want to appear to you."

Rosmarie was taken aback. Her grandmother suddenly seemed wide awake. She did not know if she had ever seen her with such presence of mind. Usually, she seemed to drift away into far away worlds and times. But now, she was present. That was exceptional.

"That the great hart appeared to the huntsman is an omen. It must be a sign for change. The sagas tell that the great spirits come to save kind people and they show up to urge the hard-hearted to care and be compassionate. Something is happening."

Rosmarie had never heard her grandmother speaking so passionately. It seemed that all the women in her family were exceptional in their own way. It seemed that they all had a connection to nature, the animals, the spiritual world, and the historical heritage of the mountain valley. To Rosmarie it felt as if this was knowledge from ancient times, from worlds before the rule of men, from nature, wisdom that was sensed not known and that was in every living creature. She could sense it. Every time one of her grandmothers or her mother started to talk with that special voice of a wise woman, she felt something moving deep inside her - something old, something ancient, something intrinsic to her that was inside her body, and it was at the same time, a connection to all the atoms in the universe. It was an embodied feeling, that filled her with unknown knowledge, that was beyond rationality, knowledge that could be only sensed through the connections of one's body to the universe. It was this sensation she had when she walked out under a full moon. It was this sensation she had when she stood barefoot in the sun-flooded forest. It was that sensation she felt when she touched an animal. It was a sense of connection, a way of knowing that there is a sensation that is called love and that is the language spoken by all creatures. But it is also knowing pain is felt by all creatures. This bodily sensation was a way of knowing that all life is connected, and that love is what makes the world brighter, and that pain is suffering, no matter how small a creature is. It was this sensation that led her on the path of care and compassion. All those who knew and truly understood shared this path.

This was what Rosmarie had learned this year. She had learned that her grandmother Frieda, as well as her mother Viktoria, walked on this path. Now she knew that her other grandmother Maria Rosa did it too. She smiled. It made her happy. She felt a deep connection to her grandmother that she had never felt before.

In exactly this moment, when Rosmarie looked at her grandmother with this sensation of being connected to her, she looked at her too. Their eyes met. Rosmarie could tell that her grandmother felt the connection as well. She smiled at Rosmarie and made an almost invisible nod by bowing her head ever so slightly. This told Rosmarie that her grandmother recognised her as one of the knowing women. She was a fellow of the great spirits. The fellows recognised each other.

THE PEGASUS

The following morning they loaded the horse into a trailer and drove down to the car ferry. Mary Rose was tense for the entire boat ride. She could not really enjoy the view over the water. She knew her horse was not comfortable being stuck in the narrow trailer, unable to move. But it was better than taking the livestock ferry.

Her heart felt heavy when she saw the white cliffs of her homeland disappearing in the mist. She was travelling ever further from home. She thought of her grandmother. She felt anxious. She only could breathe properly and relax when they were finally on the other side of the channel and she could get her horse out of the trailer. She sighed. They made it to France.

Mary Rose was glad that the crossing of the channel had been without incident. She thanked Lady Sally and continued her ride. The landscape was beautiful here and Mary Rose hoped it would help her and her horse begin to relax once more. They were both a bit exhausted with the horse trudging along listlessly. Mary Rose started to sing, partially through relief. The shock of the events in the harbour town had been draining and they needed some time to regain their spirits. On the one hand, she was grateful that they had crossed the channel safely. On the other hand, she was still disturbed about the slaughter house and those men. She felt somehow guilty, and it was difficult to look at her horse, knowing she was not able to explain to it why some of her species treated animals like that and why she was powerless against it.

Their dampened mood lingered, even though the sun shone and it was nice and warm. Mary Rose got off the horse and walked for a couple of hours. This helped to clear her mind and relieve some of the tension. Soon they came to a beautiful meadow at the edge of a forest. She stopped to let the horse graze for a while. She lay in the sun, hoping to restore her energy. Presently she started riding again and asked for a slow trot. They needed to make up some distance now, otherwise they would not reach the stable before darkness. Their mood was getting slightly better. Mary Rose had the feeling the horse was over it, but she still felt a heaviness in her heart. They managed to reach the stable just before dusk fell and Mary Rose was relieved to find herself back on schedule.

The next few days and nights passed smoothly and uneventfully. They made their daily distance and reached the stables before darkness. France was beautiful and the people were friendly. Her hosts always invited her for dinner, which almost always consisted of three courses and excellent wine. These people knew how to live well. At dinner with an elderly couple one night, she told them the story of her grandmother, and why she needed to ride across Europe and return the gift to her grandmother's saviour. The elderly couple took each other's hands and looked at each other.

"What a wonderful story! It is so wonderful that you are doing this! The young people today sometimes do not really know, what matters anymore. At least, we sometimes get this impression. It is all about money, glamour, prestige, being fashionable and famous, rather than being true and honest. It is not about real love, it seems to be all about the illusion that is created in the internet. When we were young, we did everything for love and honour. The young people of today, we feel sometimes that they do not really care for anything, but their pictures in the internet. But you have shown us, that this is not always true. There are still some young people who care. And more than this, you do everything for what you believe in. Your grandmother must be very proud of you."

Mary Rose was left feeling wonderful after this dinner. The next morning she started riding with new energy. The ride through the beautiful French landscape was enjoyable but one day, Mary Rose began to feel like she was being followed. When she turned around in the saddle, she thought she saw a shape of a horse and a rider beneath the trees on a hillside.

'Don't be paranoid,' she said to herself and continued her ride.

A day later, she stopped her horse in the forest to graze, and leaned her back against a tree trunk, when suddenly her horse lifted its head, its ears twitched. She looked in the direction of the horse's gaze, and she saw a silhouette of a dark horse disappearing beneath the tree trunks. Mary Rose grew nervous. Was somebody following her after all? She sprang to her feet. She could not see the shape anymore, so she saddled her horse and started to ride. Every now and then she stopped and looked around observing the surroundings. The path wound through a beautiful forest, but Mary Rose was preoccupied thinking of how she could get rid of her possible shadow. She did not like being followed by a shadow, not knowing whether or not it wished her harm. She did not want to wait, until she met it either. So she needed to shake it off.

She let the horse drop down in a walk. Suddenly the forest ended, and she was looking over a wide, open plain. On the horizon, she saw more forest. She looked around. She could not see or hear any sign of the shadowy figure. It had either gone or it wanted to keep in cover, which meant it did its job well. It was impossible to cross this plain without being seen. It was wide, open land; a few kilometres down the first trees and hills rose on the other side of the flat grassland. One would have to ride straight through the open land, or make a lengthy detour around the plain along the edges of the forest. Crossing the plain left Mary Rose exposed, but would also force any followers to reveal themselves. This way, at least, she would find out if somebody was following her. The follower would have to cross the plain as well, or otherwise would lose track of her. She decided to go for it.

She let her horse speed up to a gallop and it ran in a

rhythmic motion. The ground was good. It was neither too hard nor soft and quite even. The horse picked up pace, seemingly it enjoyed the run. They set off across the plain in a fast gallop leaving a cloud of dust behind. In the middle of the plain, she turned around in the saddle and looked back. She could not see anybody following. She was relieved, but still she did not feel sure enough to relax. The horse ran ever faster and she let it run as fast as it wanted.

The horse's hooves were like thunder on the ground. The ground shook as the thunder grew louder, harder, and faster. When she looked up, she realised the sky was blue and wide. Then, all of a sudden, she did not hear the thunder anymore. The rhythmic movement of the gallop turned into a flow. The horse was going so fast that it wasn't galloping anymore, but floating. The movement was even. It was as if an airplane was taking off - loud and bumpy at first, but then suddenly smooth and even. That was the moment she could feel the horse taking off. They were flying. The horse had become a Pegasus. It had spread its invisible wings. The horse was flying across the plain. Mary Rose loved to fly on the back of her horse.

When they reached the trees, the horse was dripping with sweat. She steered it behind some trees and bushes and observed the plain. Nothing happened. She waited. After a few minutes, the silhouette of a dark horse and its rider appeared between the trees. It set off across the plain in a gallop. Mary Rose was worried. But she reminded herself that she was a knight of the unicorn. She took a deep breath and let her horse continue through the forest in a fast trot. Soon, she saw a stream that ran through the forest. This gave her an idea. She would try her grandmother's trick. At the riverbed, she steered the horse into the muddy ground, and then rode into the water. She rode out of the river on the other side to make sure she left hoof-prints on the muddy riverbed. Hundred meters down she left the road by jumping over some bushes next to the road. She rode the horse across the forest until she found a good hiding place. There she waited with the horse quietly.

After a while she heard hoofbeats. They clattered along the road straight into the stream, where they stopped for a while. Then the clip-clop of the clattering hooves continued along the road. Mary Rose was glad. She sighed. She was relieved. The trick must have worked. The pursuer must have thought she had crossed the river on the other side and continued riding along the path. She let the horse graze for a while. Eventually, she continued to ride. She remained alert. The horse sensed it and was alert too. Its ears were constantly moving and listening to the sounds of the forest. Mary Rose was peering through the trees on the lookout for her pursuer. She had to be careful. If the pursuer stopped to rest she could ride straight into them.

Then she got a glimpse through the dense forest into a clearing. For a second she saw a horse. Mary Rose stopped and held her breath. The horse was grazing on its own. Where was the rider? She read the expression of her horse and its ear movements. They indicated something off to their right-hand side. Then she heard a branch cracking. It was close to them. It must be just beside the road. She held her breath and remained motionless. She held both hands underneath her coat, one on her dagger, the other on her bow. A person in a long coat came out of the bushes, crawling through the undergrowth, possibly looking for mushrooms.

Mary Rose and her horse stood a few meters down the road. "Who are you and why are you following me?" Mary Rose spoke out loud.

The person froze for a moment, and then started to turn around slowly.

FOR THE TRUST OF A HORSE

"Where is the great hart? It used to come and visit us every once in a while, but I have not seen it in a while," grandmother Maria Rosa said.

Rosmarie sighed deeply. She still wanted the huntsman to pay for that. Was it enough that he wanted to change? Was that the purpose? Was it true that the great hart was only seen if it wanted to be seen? Had it appeared to the huntsman as an omen? Had it sacrificed its life? Had it been willing to die, just to change this one man? Maybe it knew its time had come and it wanted to leave a message behind? It had walked up to the raised hide and waited until the huntsman shot it. But he had not hit it properly. Or was it not a coincidence? Did it have another purpose in mind, to reunite the three women of the family, and revive the fellowship of the unicorn? Either way, it was hard for Rosmarie to accept.

"I am afraid that it did not survive the winter."

They all sighed sadly.

"But yesterday, I went for a stroll in the forest and I saw hinds with fawns. Some were brown-red and one was fiery-red."

Maria Rosa smiled. "That is wonderful."

"Did you know that the great hart is the emblem of Erhard's family? They used to be hunters. Your grandfather was the first one who quit hunting and became a forester, a gardener, and a farmer."

"Why? What happened?"

"He also had a vision. He saw the unicorn. That changed his life."

Erhard muttered:

"No. I changed. And I saw a horse in the forest. That is coincidence, not the cause."

Maria Rosa just smiled at Rosmarie.

"What? You saw the unicorn? Tell me everything about it!"

"It was no unicorn. It was a horse. There are no unicorns," Erhard muttered.

He got up and went outside to chop wood for the stove. He was going to cook dinner. The cabin had no electricity. They were still living as they always had; one needed to chop wood and make a fire if one wanted to cook.

"Grandma! Tell me!" Rosmarie was excited.

"Come, I'll show you something. Take me to the shed, darling Rosmarie," grandmother Maria Rosa said.

Rosmarie pushed her grandmother's wheelchair to the shed next to the house where hay and wood was stored. Grandfather Erhard finished chopping wood and went inside the house to light a fire. Rosmarie opened the door of the shed and pushed the wheelchair inside.

There was an almost magical atmosphere in here. The shed was stuffed with hay and wood piles that reached right up to the roof. Through small windows rays of sunlight fell into the shed and filled the room with warm, golden light. It smelled of wood and resin, herbs and hay. It was a normal hay shed at first sight.

Maria Rosa pointed to a wood stack on the left side. "If you pull the wooden poles at the bottom the wood stack moves."

Rosmarie did what she was told and found she could move the whole wood stack. Behind the pile was a door that was almost invisible since it was made from the same old wood as the wall. Rosmarie reached for the top of the wall where she found a wooden bar. In a small crack in between was a lever. She pulled it and the door swung open. Inside was a little chamber, stuffed with paintings and painting equipment. She saw a wooden frame with a painting on it that looked unfinished. It showed the Towers in the sunlight. It was beautiful. Rosmarie took one painting after another out of the chamber. Each painting was more beautiful than the next. The paintings showed the forest in spring, in summer, in autumn and in winter; the Towers in all seasons; a deer; birds; a squirrel; a hare; grandfather Erhard in his youth, and another where he already had a white beard; father Engelbert as a baby, a child and a young man; Senta - Grandfather's old poodle; flowers; herbs; mushrooms; the river; the view over the valley; the sky; the cabin in the snow; Engelbert and Viktoria with Rosmarie as a baby; Rosmarie as a child; Rosmarie as a young woman; and a white horse in the deep green forest.

All of the paintings were so amazing, so beautiful, so real - no, more than real, they were almost alive, they had a spirit, a breath of magic to them that made them vivid and filled with enchantments. Rosmarie knew nobody else who could paint like that. She stood in silence for a long time admiring the paintings.

"Grandma, you are a gifted painter. I will organise a private viewing for you - in the hay shed and in the forest. These paintings are so beautiful, you must share them with the world!"

Maria Rosa smiled gratefully.

"You painted the forest and the animals - the great spirits, and our family. That is wonderful."

"You paint what you love."

"And the horse? Tell me about the horse grandma. I am crazy about horses. I must have one one day."

Grandmother Maria Rosa sighed.

"Oh well! Horses are the most wonderful creatures on Earth. And we are passionate about them. We love them for being all we desire: they are wild spirits, they are a symbol of freedom, they are loyal till death. They are the best friends to have. If we earn their trust, they carry us into their world and allow us to fly with them. If they connect to you and truly trust you, you have earned a friend for life."

She paused for a while, and it seemed that her mind was wandering far into the past. Then she continued to speak:

"To be trusted by a horse is a special honour for us humans. The horse is such a wonderful creature - it is so strong and yet so kind, it is so powerful and yet so gentle, it is so free spirited and yet so connected, it is so wild and yet so social. We might feel we do not deserve their love. If we stand in front of a horse, we perceive how big it is, how strong, how fast it can run, and that it is superior to us in so many ways. And even though the horse is honest and strong, and we humans are often selfish, disloyal, small and weak, they regard us with interest and they treat us with respect. Many of us humans do not deserve that. But maybe this is how horses make humans better? Because they treat people as they ought to be and thus show them how to become a better person."

Grandmother Maria Rosa paused for a while. Her fingers brushed gently over the painting with the horse. Then she said: "If you receive the trust of a horse, you will do anything you can for it. You will do anything you can to not disappoint its trust. You know you are honoured to receive the trust of a creature so honest. You want to reciprocate and want to prove that you are worthy of being trusted. You want to show that your love is not negotiable and unconditional. You want to be there for the horse at all times and protect it from the harsh human world in which a horse has no rights. You want to give something back for all the wonders your horse has shown you, for it has carried you through an enchanted world and through the harshest storms without ever letting you down. You want to protect it, and guide it through the cruel human world in return. But sometimes there are times when you cannot even protect your own life and you cannot protect your horse. There have been bad times, cruel times, wars. War is the worst time on Earth. It was not only the horses that were treated as if they were lifeless goods, worked to death, killed and eaten - women were also treated like they were meat - many of them were raped and abused, and humans of other ethnicities or beliefs were killed and thrown away, as if they were waste. In such a time, when the world is out of control, when war destroys everything, and fear and cruelty rules, then you might not be able to guarantee your horse's safety anymore. You might not even be able to stay safe yourself. In those times, when everybody's life is at stake, when everybody is scared and threatened, only the bravest, the kindest, and those who really love honestly will choose to remain caring and compassionate for others. In those times, however, you might have to let go of what you love most. Saving lives, saving love, and refusing to stop seeing the good in the world are the most important things of all."

Maria Rosa had spoken in the whispered voice of a storyteller. She was still staring at the picture. Rosmarie was baffled. What was she talking about? In that moment Rosmarie realised the depths of the untold story hidden inside her grandmother. She had always been seen as the absent minded dreamer in a wheelchair. But she had a great talent for painting, and she had a strong spirit. Rosmarie held her breath and hoped that her grandmother would continue to speak. But the flood of words had ended. Her grandmother put the painting down and sank back in her wheelchair. Her face looked tired all of a sudden. Rosmarie wanted to hear more, but she knew that her grandmother was exhausted now.

"Thank you for telling me this. You know so much. I want to learn more from you. Maybe we can come back here tomorrow. You could show me how to paint a horse and maybe you will want to tell me more."

Grandmother Maria Rosa nodded.

Rosmarie pushed her wheelchair back to the house. It was getting dark. The nights up here in the mountains were always chilly, even at this time of the year. She shivered when she stepped out. But the smoke from the chimney was a welcome sign that grandfather Erhard had started a fire, and that it would be nice and warm inside. Maybe there was soup and hot tea as well, if they were lucky. She pushed the wheelchair along the path and looked around. The night was beautiful. The sky was starlit. The mountains rose high up into the sky. It was silent and it was dark. Rosmarie loved the nights up here, but now she was looking forward to some tea and soup. She felt a bit exhausted too. All those exciting stories made her tired.

She opened the door and pushed the wheelchair inside the house. It was nice and warm. It smelled of soup and herbal tea. Rosmarie smiled. She felt so at home up here. It was so cosy in this small house in the forest. The table was set with everything they had. They ate a nutritious soup of barley, beans and chickpeas. There was bread, cheese, eggs, pickled vegetables, and fresh salad that grandfather Erhard had harvested from his glasshouse. Then grandfather Erhard got a bottle of schnapps and a bottle of wine. He poured a shot and a glass of red wine for everybody. They raised their glasses for a toast.

THE SAGA OF THE RETURN

*T*he person turned around slowly. Underneath the hood of the long brown coat Mary Rose recognised the face. She had seen those yellow eyes before. It was Tsura, the woman who worked at the animal shelter. Mary Rose was surprised and a bit relieved, but confused at the same time.

"Speak! Why do you follow me?" She said that in a calm, but confident voice.

"I am not following you. I am just going the same way. Well, part of the way," Tsura replied.

Mary Rose was not satisfied with the answer. She stared at her with her most threatening look, but did not say a word.

"I am riding home. I want to bring a message to my grandmother who lives in the East. She is old and ill, and I want to let her know that the unicorn returned."

"What? Don't give me these riddles. Speak to me in a way I can understand." Mary Rose was harsh. She was angry. Why was this person following her? She had unnerved Mary Rose, she had expended a lot of energy from her horse trying to shake her off. Most importantly, she had wasted this energy that might be needed to complete the rest of their journey. She wanted answers.

"In our family clan there is a saga. It tells that war devastated Europe and sent it into a dismal era. Many people died, and the natural world was devastated. Many people fled, as did many animals. The saga says that there are great spirits - in old trees, but also in animals: deer, horses, and birds. The white horse is the protector of peace. If it leaves, the dreariness expands. The saga says that only when the great spirits return will there be hope for a new age. - Now the white horse has been seen, and it is on its way back to its native forests. This is a great message that must be spread all over Europe. It must be carried across the plains and the mountains, the forests and the rivers and allowed to reverberate into the sky. All the peoples and all the animals must hear and see it. Then the world will be ready for a new dawn."

Mary Rose was baffled and lost for words. She sighed and scratched her head. 'Alright,' she thought. 'Now this is getting too mystical, even for me. A saga about the return of the unicorn? Is that possible?' But hadn't her grandmother told her a similar story? She thought about the words of her grandmother that resembled this saga:

'Once great spirits roamed the forests of the Earth. Once, wild women lived in the forests of the world. War destroyed everything, killed humans and animals, and left behind nothing but devastated land, poverty, and mourning. The great spirits have to come back - the white horse known as the unicorn, the old stag known as the great hart, the great oaks, the beech tree, the pine tree and the birch tree, the deer, the rabbits, the squirrels, the birds and the bears, the wolves and the foxes, the wild women and all the human folk. Then the world would be in balance and in peace.'

Now, the white horse was returning. She liked the idea that she was the knight of the unicorn, who had a mission to return the unicorn to the forest in which its ancestors once lived. If she thought about it, it sounded very magical and also very beautiful. The purpose of her mission was to return a gift, a favour and the love received from a stranger, but somehow suddenly it was more than that.

She smiled hesitantly. "Well, I am not entirely sure about your saga, but I would like to believe it. I want to believe that there will come an era of peace and that all the creatures can live in peace. One day, hopefully, this will happen. What could one wish for more than peace on Earth? I cannot promise that we will make your saga come true, but I do promise, that I will carry the torch of love wherever I go."

They gently bowed in front of each other with their one hands on their hearts. It was a sign of mutual respect and understanding, showing that they knew what they were talking about. Even though they had lived in different places and belonged to different peoples, they spoke the same language, they told similar stories and they were on similar missions. There was something that connected all the creatures. It was love. A love that was not focused on one person, but was a love that was all-embracing. This love had been chased away by the war and it had been hiding in secret places. Now it was time for it to come back and spread all over Europe. The message was carried across the land, across the mountains and it would reverberate into the sky. Slowly, Mary Rose started to understand that this mission was greater than she had thought.

That evening, she wrote a letter to her grandmother. She wanted to tell her what had happened, that she had met a woman whose family had a saga about the unicorn whereby she was convinced that she - Mary Rose, her granddaughter - was the one who would accompany the return of the unicorn. It made her smile and it made her proud. She knew that her grandmother would love to hear this. Hopefully, she thought, that would make her happy and give her strength to stay on Earth for a little bit longer.

They continued their ride together. The coming days they rode side by side at a comfortable pace across France. The country was beautiful, sunny and full of vineyards, apple trees and golden fields. They enjoyed each other's company, shared stories. They became good friends on their way.

The mountains on the horizon were looming closer each day. When they reached Switzerland, their routes diverged. Mary Rose wanted to cross the mountains from Switzerland to Austria, which was a difficult and exhausting path. But the settlement of Tsura's family was in another direction. Saying goodbye was hard for both of them. They took each other in their arms.

"Take care. Stay safe. It was great to meet you," Mary Rose said.

"The pleasure is all mine. It was a great honour to

ride with you. Take care. Stay safe. Shine your light for all the people of the world." Tsura waved goodbye. She smiled, as one can only smile from the depth of one's heart.

Mary Rose was touched. She waved goodbye as well. They rode their separate ways.

THE HARBINGER

*R*osmarie woke at dawn. She looked out of the window. It was foggy. Her mind felt a bit foggy too, she was not used to drinking wine and schnapps. She went downstairs and saw her grandfather and her grandmother at the window looking out at something.

"It is here," Maria Rosa said. "The fiery fawn has come!"

Rosmarie stood next to them and looked for the fawn.

"It is an omen," grandmother Maria Rosa said. "It is the harbinger."

"What does it mean?" Rosmarie asked.

"Something is going to happen soon, something of great importance."

The deer were grazing on the meadow at the edge of the forest. It was a beautiful scene.

"It is such a wonderful scene. These graceful animals

in this picturesque landscape would be a good subject for your next painting grandma. Can you paint it please? And can you show me how to paint a horse?"

Grandmother Maria Rosa smiled. She loved that her granddaughter wanted to do something with her and that she could teach her something. It made her happy. Her face lit up. Erhard noticed it as well. He smiled thankfully at Rosmarie. Rosmarie noticed that it might be sometimes hard for him to get through to his wife and he was grateful that Rosmarie had found a way to make her smile. She seemed unusually excited and present this morning. Maybe it was the fawn, maybe it was painting with her granddaughter. Either way, it was a pleasant day for all of them.

After breakfast, they fetched the paint and canvas from the shed. The fog dissipated, and there was a little bit of sunshine. Rosmarie enjoyed painting with her grandmother very much. Maria Rosa painted the fiery fawn and its mother in the forest. Rosmarie painted a white horse following the instructions of her grandmother. She also drew the woman from her dream, and the coastal landscape and the sea and the sky. To her own surprise, she seemed to have inherited some of her grandmother's talent. It was actually quite good. She was wondering how she did not discover her love for painting earlier, not to mention her grandmother's passion for it. Recently, everything seemed to be miraculous to Rosmarie. Even Erhard joined them and he painted the great hart. They had a wonderful time together.

Around lunchtime it started raining. Rosmarie had to go back to the alpine hut, since she was working that evening. It was going to be a busy night as there was an engagement party up there in the afternoon. As much as she would have liked to stay for longer, she could not take the day off. She promised her grandparents that she would come back soon and continue painting. Somehow, she was suddenly very eager to paint. She had discovered a talent and a passion she had not really known about before. In school, drawing had bored her because she never liked to draw the things they were told to draw. But now she wanted to paint all the wonderful things she had encountered. She wanted to paint her mother and the great hart, her grandmother Frieda and her wolf-dog, and grandmother Maria Rosa with the fawn under her favourite tree. She began to think about giving the paintings as Christmas presents. She was thinking of what she could paint for Viktor. Maybe him and his best cow, which had won so many prizes? For Erhard, she could paint him and his poodle. For father Engelbert, she could paint him and his rabbit that he loved as a child.

It made her excited to think about what wonderful presents these would be. But if she wanted to paint so many pictures, she would have to paint regularly. So she would come back soon, maybe the following day. She had the weekend off and she wanted to spend it with her grandparents. It had been so nice with them she suddenly could not understand why she had not visited them for so long. Well, sometimes her grandmother had phases where she was really introverted and difficult to talk to. Erhard said that she sometimes dwelt on the past and that one needed to find ways to bring her into the present. It was not always easy - not only did he care for her, but also sometimes it was difficult to get through to her. Whenever Rosmarie asked him what had happened, he responded that the past was the past and one needed to let it be so. Just like Viktor, Rosmarie thought. In a way those two men were so similar.

She said she wanted to come back the next day. Her grandparents were happy about that. She said goodbye to her grandmother and was accompanied by her grandfather and his poodle down to the ravine. Then she walked back up towards the Towers. She was deep in thought. She thought indeed it was a time when things were changing. In the past few months, so many things had changed. Most of all her relationship to her mother and both of her grandmothers had improved massively. How could she not know how much depth they had, what secrets they kept, and what stories they knew? But then, she realised, she had never asked.

But there were still pieces missing from the puzzle. Viktor and Erhard were still irreconcilable. Her father Engelbert had turned his back on them, because he was annoyed with their feuding. Was there a way to bring them back together, and unite the whole family? It would require a miracle. She could not think of anything that would bring them all together - maybe her funeral, she thought, with a sardonic laugh to herself. But that was too early at this point in her life. She felt that she only now had discovered the secrets of life, and she was hungry for more. Now, that she was eighteen, life offered new and exciting possibilities for her.

'The horse,' she thought, 'I need a horse. But can I handle a horse and study at the same time? And work and be a guardian?' Somehow she would manage. She needed to trust in her abilities.

The evening was busy. There were many more guests than the mountain restaurant was equipped for. She helped with cooking and preparing food throughout the afternoon, and she had to serve at high speed. It was busy all afternoon, and in the evening, people wanted to start leaving. Rain was pouring down outside. Little waterfalls were falling from the gutters. People were worried about going down the ravine in this weather. The landlord said it was dangerous. They would have to stay for the night and go down in the morning.

The rain poured all through the night, and had still not let up the following morning. People at breakfast seemed not to know what to do. Some begged the landlord to drive them down to the valley. He refused, explaining that it was dangerous even by car. A few hours later the rain suddenly stopped. Eventually, the landlord agreed to drive a single car load of people.

"But only because we ran out of salad and vegetables, after people ate so much last night," the cook whispered to Rosmarie.

The landlord drove off, but less than an hour later, they were back again. The torrent had turned into a thunderous stream, it was so full of water that big waves were crashing across the bridge over the ravine. The route down was impassable.

THE MOUNTAIN PASS

*I*n Switzerland, Mary Rose and her horse started to climb the mountains that bordered with Austria. It was a stony and steep path. They had to go slowly, being careful and attentive. Mary Rose worried about her horse's legs and hooves on the stony, uneven ground. Now that they were so close to their destiny, she would have loved to go there at a canter. But the mountain terrain was no racing ground. It was steep, rocky, and tricky. She let the horse decide how fast it wanted to go. They had been climbing uphill all morning. They had ridden past many old farmsteads, built in the traditional way, with a stone fundament and the rest made from wood. Many people came out of their houses and watched their appearance. Wherever they went, people came to admire them.

Was it true? Was the saga of the unicorn real? It seemed that all the people sensed something. Maybe subconsciously they knew. Why would they come and watch otherwise? They sensed that something was going on - magic was happening, legends were coming true, the unicorn was returning.

The road led up and up, and the mountains seemed endless. They had looked huge from far away. But now that she was close, she fully realised just how big those mountains really were. The Alps! There were some peaks that still had snow on their tops. They were majestic, towering rock walls, that reached high up into the sky. Mary Rose hoped that the pass across to Austria was not too stony or too steep, and that the horse would manage to get there without incidents. The road grew steeper, but even on these steep hills there were still houses and people who made these slopes their homes. It was amazing, Mary Rose thought.

Around lunchtime, they reached the forest. Mary Rose stopped the horse and let it graze. She let herself fall into the grass and stretched. Her body was sore from the long ride and she was tired of travelling. She dozed off.

"Look mum, a unicorn!"

Mary Rose woke with a start. She sat up and looked around. She spotted her horse standing with its front legs up on a rock, stretching its neck to the top of the rock to reach some herbs. A group of hikers with several children had stopped nearby and they were all watching the horse. They had not discovered Mary Rose who was sitting in the high grass. Mary Rose smiled.

'Smart child,' she thought. 'At least one human who recognises a unicorn when she sees one.'

One of the children said: "There are no unicorns, that is just a fairy tale."

The other child said: "Are you blind? Look at it. This is a real unicorn."

"Unicorns exist only in magic wonderlands," the other child said.

The lady replied: "Those who don't believe in magic will not find it."

Then the group of hikers continued descending the mountain. It took a while for Mary Rose to get up and stretch her aching legs. Then she got on her horse and continued to ride towards the mountain pass.

The morning had been nice and sunny. But now she noticed dark clouds. She needed to get on with the ascent - no more breaks. Bad weather was coming. She asked the horse to pick up its pace. She knew the ground would get slippery when it was wet and that was dangerous on such a steep path. The horse walked faster, up, up, up. After a while she felt a wind coming up. She turned around in the saddle and looked back. The clouds were coming up quickly behind her. A harsh wind was blowing up the hillsides ahead of them. It did not look good at all. Mary Rose knew how dangerous a storm in the mountains could be. She began to think about turning back but she could already see the pass up ahead. That must be the Tower Gate. She was so close. Maybe she would reach a safe place faster on the other side of the pass than if she turned back now. It had been a four hour ride since the last Alpine hut. Plus the horse was faster walking uphill than downhill. Maybe she should press ahead.

It started raining moments later. To begin with, it was drizzling. They finally reached the pass to Austria: the Tower Gate. Mary Rose sighed. She felt relieved. The view from here must be exhilarating if the weather were nicer, she thought. For now it was just clouds. The rain was getting heavier so she pushed on without a break. The path turned downhill on the other side. She got off the horse and walked beside it. It was slippery and they had to move slowly. The rain came down more and more heavily. Mary Rose began to worry. The clouds were hanging low - or was it fog?

'Oh no,' she thought. 'Please, not fog while we are up here. Hopefully we won't get lost.'

The fog got thickened quickly. Soon she could not see more than a few metres ahead. She was already wet and hungry, and now she was scared. She watched her footing carefully, trying desperately not to lose the path. She rubbed her eyes and tried to be alert. The fog was thick. The wind was getting harsher and the rain was lashing down. Mary Rose was wet to the skin. The fear crawled up into her bones. She knew they could die here in the mountains and they would probably not be found until days later. They moved very slowly, struggling to see anything. The wind blew the rain horizontally across the landscape. She could hardly keep her eyes open.

Suddenly the horse stopped. It lifted its head and it seemed to smell something. Then it walked off the road onto a very narrow beaten path that was barely visible. It led through a few big trees into a clearing. In the clearing, behind the trees, they found a shed. The horse walked straight towards it. Mary Rose looked through gaps in its tree trunk walls and saw it was stuffed with hay.

"You, you saved us," she told the horse.

She needed some force to open the door. She tied a

rope to it and had the horse pull, and as soon as the door swung open, they both ran into the dry hay shed. She closed the door behind them. The storm howled outside, but inside it was cosy. The shed was protected in a hollow with a clump of trees, and the walls were made from big, thick tree-trunks that kept the storm outside.

Mary Rose was so relieved that they were safe. She dropped her things on the floor. She took the saddle from the horse's back and rubbed the horse dry with bundles of hay. Then she took off all her clothes and hung them up to dry. She only had a warm blanket to wear, that she had kept in a dry bag, so she dug herself a nest in the hay and lay down. The horse had plenty to eat. She had some nuts left in her bag which she nibbled. It was surprisingly warm and cosy in the hay. She fell asleep with the storm howling the whole night and rain lashing outside the shed. But she felt safe in here. She woke up several times to check on the horse. It was still chewing on the hay. It must have been very hungry, she thought. But also the hay smelled very good. The mountain herbs gave it a special smell.

'We were lucky,' Mary Rose thought before she fell asleep again.

IN THE RAVINE

*G*randmother Frieda called. She said that grandfather Viktor had wanted to stay in the mountain cabin the evening before. So she and uncle Vinzent had driven down to the valley without him. They had only heard about the storm warning when they watched the news in the evening. That morning, they drove back up to look after grandfather Viktor but the bridge over the ravine was impassable. The torrent was thunderous and the water was crashing over the sides of the bridge. It was just a matter of time until the bridge was torn away by the torrent. Frieda asked Rosmarie to go and check in on grandfather Viktor. She tried to speak in a calm and confident voice, but Rosmarie sensed the worry in her grandmother's voice. She was worried. She had a sense for things. Rosmarie knew that it was serious.

Rosmarie started walking straight away. It was still raining and it was chilly. She felt uneasy. She had a bad feeling in her stomach. She grew more and more nervous, and eventually she broke into run. She ran all the way down. As she ran, she began to remember scenes from her childhood. Back then, when she was a child, grandfather Viktor used to be able to go for walks. He had taken her to the alpine hut, and he had told her stories on the way. Somehow she had forgotten about them, and now all of a sudden the memory came flooding back to her. She ran past the rock walls that glowed yellow, golden, and red in the evening, when the dwarves lit their fire up there. They were underground during the day and came out in the evening. She ran through the forest where the pixies lived, that made the sparkling snow crystals for Christmas. She ran down the steep rocky path beneath the big boulders, that were trolls that were petrified by the sun. Some of them had slept for so long that moss and trees grew on them. Others awakened in the dark, and they ate children who were disobedient and went out in the dark forest on their own. She ran down the hill to the cabin, where a herd of goats and sheep lived with a herdsman with a long white beard, who was more than hundred years old and whose best friend was a tree of the age of seven hundred years. People said he would live as long as the tree was alive. She ran through the woodland with the once murmuring torrent which had now become a swollen river overnight. At the point where one could cross the torrent, one needed to watch out for the merman, who fished with his trident for people who were inattentive or disrespectful, and particularly those who threw their rubbish in the water. She ran across the meadow with the stone-wall, where the marmots lived, who guarded over the valley and whistled when strangers came. Their alarm whistle was so loud that the whole valley knew. She ran past the lodge and the cabins on the lower pastures, and finally she could see her grandparents' alpine cabin.

The cows were in the shed. They watched her through the windows as she came closer. She ran into the house. The door was unlocked, nobody was there. She ran back to the shed and counted the cows.

"Damn it!" She cursed out loud.

One was missing. It must be one of the youngsters. It had probably got lost in the rain and the storm, and Viktor had gone to look for it. She could imagine him walking with his stick and his monocle to look for the cow. He was a stubborn old man. But where did he go?

"Where did he go?" She asked the cows.

The cows looked at her, and then they looked towards the ravine.

"Oh no," she said.

She ran towards the ravine. Her heart was beating heavily. She held her breath when she looked down into the ravine. The water was wild. At this point, the ravine was not as deep as it was further down where the bridge was. It was much broader and some trees were growing on both sides. Usually one could even cross it. But this time she could already hear the roaring river. The water was much higher than usual. It had torn away whole trees, which had begun to form a dam. The whole ford was flooded. Then she saw the cow that was stuck on an island, formed by a small hill with a tree. It was scared of going into the raging torrent. Grandfather Viktor was stuck at the steep wall of the ravine. It looked like he had fallen and was injured.

"Grandpa! I am here! I'm coming for you. Hold on!"

Rosmarie shouted as loud as she could. She saw her grandfather's head moving a tiny little bit. She was relieved. He was still alive. With shaking hands she grasped her phone and called Erhard. He said he would come right away. He knew a path through the wood, where he would not have to cross the torrent. But it would take a while.

Then she ran back to the house and looked for a rope. She found two in the shed and an old harness that had been used for the working ox that pulled the plough before her uncle bought a tractor. She took that too. Maybe it would be good for her grandfather to hold on to. His hands were not so strong anymore so he probably could not hold on to a rope.

She hurried back. She tied one end of the rope to a tree, and threw the other end with the harness down to Viktor, but he was not able to pull it over him. He must have been in the ice-cold water for a while as he seemed to not have the strength to hold on with one arm whilst pulling the harness over with the other. At the same time Rosmarie knew she was not strong enough to pull him up the vertical wall. She grew desperate. What should she do? She lost all hope for a moment, until another idea came to her. She tied the other rope to a tree further down at the ford, where the ravine was broader and flatter. She wanted to fight her way up through the ice-cold water, grab her grandfather and climb out onto the flat part. Could she do that? Her grandfather was quite heavy. He could not hold on to the rope. If she lost him, he would die. A new plan came to her mind. She would tie herself to both ropes. She would abseil down the vertical wall directly above the spot where Viktor was. She would put him into the harness and tie him to the rope. Then she would fight her way down the torrent and jump out at the flat spot. And by the time hopefully Erhard arrived and helped her pull Viktor up.

Carefully she abseiled down and she managed to get all the way to her grandfather. When she reached him, his lips were blue and his body ice-cold. She put the harness over him and tied one of the ropes to it firmly. Then she climbed along the rocks to the spot where the ravine was flat. Ice-cold water washed around her feet. Every now and then a wave jumped at her, and almost washed her off the wall. She was wet to her bones. She made one careful step after the other. She tested each hold and each step before she put her weight on it. She traversed slowly along the rock wall. She was almost there. She was close to the ford. In that moment, a massive wave jumped off the boulders, right onto Rosmarie. The huge wall of water washed her right off the rock and away with the floods.

Ice cold water hit Rosmarie. Her head was pressed under water. She paddled for her life. She managed to reach the surface and catch a breath before the next wave crashed into her face. With a jerk, the rope tightened. She had to paddle with both arms to keep her head above the water. So she had no chance to grab the rope and pull herself towards the bank. The stream was so strong and so wild, she had no chance. Was she going to die in the ravine? Was that her fate? Why? Why was the ravine so merciless? Wasn't she too young to die? There were so many things she wanted to do. Was this what would bring her family back together after all? Her funeral? This wasn't what she had wished for when she had seen a shooting star up in the night sky. Maybe one could only wish for something, but needed to leave it to fate to decide how it would happen?

Ice-cold water was streaming over Rosmarie's body. She knew, she would not be able to keep her head above the water for much longer. Thunderous water was roaring around her.

'I am going to die,' Rosmarie thought.

Her body was ice-cold, wet, frozen, she was scared and she could hardly keep her head up long enough to breathe. What should she do? Just wait until she died? Was this the end? Rosmarie closed her eyes for a moment.

THE ARRIVAL

*I*n the morning it was still raining. But the fog was lifting. Mary Rose studied her map and tried to get some reception on her navigation system. If the satnav was correct, they were actually quite close to their destination. About two hours' ride from here - depending on the ground and the weather conditions - there was a big mountain hut, which provided shelter for hikers. Right beside it was a farmstead, that provided shelter for the animals that spent the summer on the alpine pastures. Further down this highland valley was the place where she wanted to be. She was nearly there! She was close to her destination. She would find a place to stay somewhere and then start her search for the woman she was looking for. She hoped that she would be able to find her.

She gently brushed her horse as it nibbled on the hay. She spoke to it.

"We have made it. We are in the highland valley

already. This is our destination. Now we just need to find her. I don't know if she is still alive, but maybe she is? Or maybe she has children and grandchildren. Can you help me find them? I know you have this sense - the special sense. Can you keep your sense sharp, and let me know if you sense her?"

The horse snorted. Mary Rose was convinced that the horse had understood her plea. She prepared the horse to continue the ride. She was glad that she made it all the way to this highland valley. She was glad that the horse had withstood the journey well. But after last night, the endless ascent, the storm, the wet, the cold and the danger, she was overall very relieved that they were here. With the end so close, she felt her exhaustion catching up with her. The horse seemed tired too. But now that she was almost there, she could take it slowly today, and find a safe place to stay until she found this woman. She saddled the horse and they started walking. Mary Rose walked beside the horse feeling chilly in her damp clothes. She had to walk to stay warm and make sure she could dry herself properly at some point. The saddle pad was soaked as well, and had barely dried overnight. Mary Rose did not want to risk bruising the horse's back. So she walked.

The horse walked purposefully in the opposite direction of to the road they had come the day before. Mary Rose followed it. She had asked it to lead, so she had to trust its judgement. The beaten path led beneath some big trees, across a meadow towards a woodland. The woodland was beautiful. The ground was dark-green, the tree trunks were a light grey and the young leaves of the tree tops were bright green. There was a little stream murmuring across the woodland. She saw some edible mushrooms and took them with her for that night's dinner. Whilst she picked the mushrooms, the horse went to the stream and drank. She observed it, she saw how it looked into the water, and noticed that there were frogs swimming in there. She saw a salamander that was black with yellow spots. This was a beautiful place, despite the rain.

Then the horse followed a beaten path through the woodland. It stopped at a big tree and its ears started moving. Mary Rose noticed that there were a lot of tiny little birds sitting in the tree. They had blue and yellow feathers. They were all looking at the white horse as it looked up at them. The horse continued to walk, and the little birds started to sing. Mary Rose smiled. The lilting melody of the bird song made her heart feel elated. She forgot about the wet clothes and the chilliness and skipped along the path, whistling the melody of the bird's song. The horse seemed to feel the vibe of the tune as well and walked with a spring in its step. It went across the woodland, crossed the stream and then stopped all of a sudden. Its attention was focused straight forward. There was a hare that looked at the horse and then hopped away. The horse paused for a moment and then went on. To the one side, the forest became very steep and the trees were growing on an almost vertical slope. At the top, above the trees, Mary Rose saw a vertical rock wall rising high up into the sky. It was a light grey in colour, and must have been several hundred metres high. The mountain scenery was impressive.

The horse continued on its way unerringly. Then it

stopped again and raised its head up high. Mary Rose noticed a herd of deer in the forest, looking at the horse. It seemed to be hinds and fawns. Most of them were red-brown, but one hind was a bright orange in colour, and one fawn was almost of a fiery orange. Mary Rose watched them with fascination. She remembered that her grandfather had once told her a story about a great hart that used to live in the forests somewhere in England, or perhaps it was Wales or Scotland. The great hart had majestic antlers it looked like it was carrying a tree on its head. Some people said that its appearance was a sign, an omen, a call. Others, ignorant and greedy people, hunted it. But nobody ever managed to kill it, despite them using horses and packs of hunting dogs. There were many legends around it. Legends told that it was a symbol of life; that it was a guardian; a messenger; that the great hart was sent from the tree of life to remind people to cherish life and the living; and that it lived in the magic forest.

Mary Rose paused and enjoyed the scenery. 'A magic forest,' she thought, 'a unicorn forest.' Suddenly she noticed that this was a wonderful forest, an enchanted forest. It was full of ancient trees and beautiful animals, all of which seemed to watch the white horse with great interest.

'Maybe, it is true,' she thought. 'Maybe, this is the return of the unicorn?' There was nothing she wanted to believe more than this. She opened her arms and spun around like a carousel. Oh, this was wonderful! She loved living in a magical story. Could it get any better than this?

They followed their path through the forest. After a

while, they rejoined the road that crossed their path and they followed it down for quite some time. It led out of the forest onto a high plain, which was a pasture for cattle. Cows were grazing all over the place. Some of them were standing on the steep hillside beneath big boulders. Apparently, cows were more sure-footed than they seemed, she thought. They crossed the plain and Mary Rose noticed a big alpine hut in the distance.

Mary Rose felt chilly and hungry. She was thinking of stopping here to get breakfast. She was starving and needed a break. She stood there and looked to the hut. Smoke was coming out of the chimney. A warm light was glowing in the windows. It smelled of cooked food. Just as she was walking towards the hut, she saw somebody coming out of the hut and setting off down the path at a fast pace. The person wore a long coat and a hood, and seemed to be in a hurry, not even noticing her and the horse approaching from the other side. Mary Rose stopped at the entrance of the hut, but the horse kept walking. It was not going to take a break here. Mary Rose was surprised. Even though she longed for hot tea and proper breakfast, she decided to follow the horse. After all, she had asked it to lead.

They followed the path downwards and it seemed they were going the same way as the person walking in front of them. 'Hold on,' Mary Rose thought. 'Maybe that is her?' Her heart jumped. Was this the woman she was searching for? Was that why the horse had kept on going? Usually it never skipped a grazing break. Was she the right one? Mary Rose got excited. She did not want to rush things in her excitement. She tried to stay calm, after all, she had no proof. She decided to see where the person was going. She kept some distance. She wanted to remain discrete.

The person was marching quickly, then started to jog, and broke into a run a moment later. The person ran sure-footedly down the uneven path, avoiding the tangled roots and slippery surfaces, jumping from one rock to the other like an ibex, and leaping over roots and across the torrent.

Mary Rose was impressed. She had never seen a human, who was so surefooted in these conditions. This person must have grown up here that was for sure. Mary Rose could not keep up. There were too many rocks and roots and she was worried that her horse could stumble and hurt its legs. It was not an ibex, after all. And she herself was not as agile on this terrain either. That moment she realised that it was very unlikely that this was the woman she was looking for because she would be the age of her grandmother and it was unlikely she could walk so fast. She was disappointed. It seemed that she would lose this person. When she came out of the forest, she saw the person had already made it down a steep hill and across the torrent, disappearing into behind the fir trees.

She allowed the horse to choose the path and pace. It should decide how fast it wanted to go in this mud and it should show her the way. After all, it was the horse's idea to follow this person. The path led down the steep hill where goats and sheep where grazing. It led through another woodland and across a torrent, then it led down a meadow with a stone-wall, where many marmots lived. They were sitting up and peering. Once they crossed the stone-wall, they arrived at a pasture with a shed. They crossed a forest of pine trees and when they left it the plain opened up into big meadows, where several alpine cabins were built. Several small paths led up to each of the cabins. At one junction the horse stopped. It lifted its head up and flared its nostrils. It sniffed the air. It snorted. Its ears were moving and indicating towards the right-hand side. It kept staring in that direction. Its nostrils were fully flared and its eyes wide open. The ears were pricked up. It was alert.

Suddenly the horse set off in a trot along the path, past an alpine cabin and a shed towards the roaring noise of a mountain river. Mary Rose ran after the horse. The horse stopped and looked down into a ravine full of wild roaring water.

THE MIRACLE

'*I* am dead,' Rosmarie thought. She was struggling to survive in the icy deluge of the water. She could hardly keep her head above the surface. She felt certain that she was doomed to die here. Then she thought she felt something. It was a feeling. A presence. What was it? Was somebody there? Was somebody coming to save her? She looked towards the bank. She saw the shape of a white horse appearing. Was she hallucinating? Was she dead? In the same moment she remembered her favourite bed time story from her childhood: the saga of the unicorn.

"Keep your heart honest and kind, and the unicorn might come to save you, when you are in great need," her grandmother had told her. Rosmarie remembered the words like it was yesterday.

She looked up again. Still she saw the shape of a white horse. She closed her eyes and opened them again. Was this real? A white horse standing at the bank looking at her. It was beautiful. She just stared at it. A person in a long coat ran towards the end of the rope. Another wave pressed Rosmarie under water. She disappeared into the depths of the icy torrent. This was the end. Her body was frozen and she had no more strength to swim. The icy cold froze her body. She knew she had no chance against the current. The ice-cold water would surely take her life. She was going to die in the wild water of the ravine.

Then she felt a hard pull and a strong pain. The rope tightened and cut into her flesh. The pain was unbearable. But Rosmarie grabbed the rope and held onto it. She held her breath and paddled with the last ounce of her strength. She fought for her life. She paddled and rose above the water's surface for a second, just long enough to gasp for some air before she was pushed back under the water.

Then it suddenly stopped. She must be dead. She opened her eyes. She looked into the dark sky. She lay on the bank. She gasped for air. She was alive! She felt dizzy and exhausted. She coughed for a while. When she opened her eyes again, she saw the sky. The clouds were dark. A long white face appeared above her.

'What is that?' Rosmarie thought.

A big nose came closer and blew its breath into her face.

Rosmarie giggled.

The big nose pushed gently against her shoulder and she rolled over.

She tried to sit up and free herself of the rope. She was freezing. The big nose came again and blew into her face. Rosmarie took it with both hands and bowed with her head. She made a reverent nod.

"Thank you for saving me," she whispered. "I owe you my life."

Then she looked up. The person under the coat was a woman. "Thank you for saving me. I owe you my life," Rosmarie said to her too.

The woman smiled. She seemed very happy and relieved that Rosmarie could still talk. She extended her a hand. "My pleasure."

Rosmarie grabbed the hand and was pulled to her feet. She pointed towards the spot where her grandfather was. The woman understood straight away. She led the horse to the other rope and tied it to the saddle. Then she asked the horse to pull whilst she also pulled with both hands on the rope. They eventually managed to pull grandfather Viktor up, who was hanging in the harness.

Rosmarie cried tears of relief. She ran to Viktor who lay on the ground and could barely move. He was not well, his lips were blue and he was shivering and he must have broken his leg. At the same moment she heard the engines of Erhard's motor bike. Rosmarie was glad he was here. He looked after Viktor, who had a broken leg and was shivering with hypothermia. He put a thick blanket around him and lifted him into the sidecar of his motorbike. He said he would take him to his place; Maria Rosa had everything prepared to give first aid. Rosmarie agreed gratefully. Her grandmother had been a nurse at one point. Grandfather Erhard provided care for grandmother Maria Rosa and was also a hobby veterinarian for his animals. He knew how to care for sick and injured people and animals. Since the ravine down to the valley and the hospital was impassable, this was the best thing to do.

The woman said she could give Rosmarie a ride and they would follow as fast as possible. But first she asked Erhard to help pulling. The woman tied the rope into a lasso and managed to throw a loop over the cow's horns. She asked Erhard and Rosmarie to help pull. Together, with their combined strength and the power of the horse, they managed to pull the cow across the raging torrent and out of the water. Once the animal was safe, Erhard drove off with Viktor in the sidecar.

Rosmarie could not take her eyes off the horse. She was so fascinated by it, she forgot that she was frozen and almost drowned. Rosmarie looked at the horse with awe. What a beautiful horse! She had never seen such a horse before. It was white with silver and golden shining on its shimmering fur.

"It is beautiful," Rosmarie stuttered. She carefully put out her hand towards the horse and remained motionless for a moment.

The horse looked at her. Then it reached its nose out to meet Rosmarie's hand and gently blew its breath on her palm. This tickled and she got goosebumps all over from the gentle touch of breath. Then she carefully tried to touch it. It let her stroke its forehead. It had no horn on its forehead, but for Rosmarie this horse was still magical, from the first time she had seen it. She was enchanted from the moment she touched it.

The woman watched the horse and Rosmarie with interest. "She likes you," she said.

Rosmarie gave her a warm smile. "Yeah, I like her too."

The woman looked at Rosmarie with a strange gaze that she could not quite interpret. It was as if there was a knowing sparkle in her eyes. She extended her hand again to Rosmarie.

"I am Mary Rose," she said.

Rosmarie was a little bit surprised at the similarity of their names.

"I am Rosmarie," she said.

Again there was a sparkle in Mary Rose's eyes that Rosmarie could not really read.

"It is a pleasure to meet you," she said. "I think we might get along well with each other. But first you should get some dry clothes and warm up. You must be freezing."

Rosmarie nodded. She quickly went inside the alpine cabin and put on some of Frieda's clothes. Then she returned.

Mary Rose made a gesture with her head and with one finger pointing, and the horse kneeled down on one leg. She sat in the saddle and held out her hand to Rosmarie. "Come on. We will give you a ride."

Rosmarie was still shivering, her teeth were chattering, and she was in pain, but she smiled when she was invited for the ride. She sat on the horse's back and it started to walk.

"You lead the way," Mary Rose said.

The horse dropped into a slow trot. It was impressively strong. Even though it was not very big, it managed to keep up the trot, despite having to carry two people up the winding path. Only when they reached the stiff peak did it slow down to a walk. After it had climbed the steepest part, it started trotting again. They crossed the woodland and the grassland with the torrent and soon she could see her grandparents' hut. The motorbike stood outside. Light shone through the windows and smoke rose from the chimney. As they crossed the meadow, the door to the terrace opened and grandmother Maria Rosa rolled out in her wheelchair.

MAGIC UNFOLDING

$\mathcal{M}$ary Rose was witnessing the magic unfolding. It was unbelievable. The arrival of the white horse changed everything. Secrets were revealed. Gratitude chased away all doubts. Worries were erased. Wounds being healed. Hope was being revived. Feuds and prejudices were buried. It was as if the light of the magic white horse shone into the dark corners of the Self, and its pure presence encouraged everybody to overcome their shadows and become the best possible Self. The world appeared in a new light. With the arrival of the white horse, a light was lit in every heart.

When the white horse with the two women on its back trotted across the meadow, the woman in the wheelchair stared at them. She could hardly trust her eyes. Was this real? Was she hallucinating? Her heart beat heavily. She was excited. She reached with her arms towards the horse and spoke out loud:

"Fortuna, is that you?"

The horse stopped right in front of her. Maria Rosa stared at the horse and then at Mary Rose. She had tears in her eyes. With shivering hands she groped for the horse's head. The horse let her touch its forehead. Maria Rosa broke out in tears. She kissed the horse's forehead. Then she looked up at Mary Rose while tears ran down her cheeks.

Mary Rose jumped off the horse. Her eyes were filled with tears as well. She fell into Maria Rosa's arms. The two hugged each other for a long time. They held each other in their arms as if they were close friends, finally reunited.

Rosmarie had no idea what had happened, but the scene was so touching that she felt overwhelmed. What was going on? How did this woman know her grandmother? How did her grandmother know this horse? Who was this woman? Why was she called the same name as her grandmother? Rosmarie was completely puzzled.

Meanwhile the two of them still held each other in their arms, as if they had been waiting for this moment for a very long time, and never wanted it to end.

Rosmarie was still sitting on the horse's back watching the scene, when she noticed that her grandfather Erhard was standing at the corner of the hut, watching. She noticed that he was deeply moved as well. Rosmarie had never seen her grandfather crying before.

Maria Rosa was still shedding tears as she looked at Mary Rose, nodded and smiled at her whilst she was crying at the same time.

Rosmarie got off the horse. She still was wondering what was going on.

Maria Rosa sat in the wheelchair, and then she folded both hands in front of her heart and bowed gently. The horse moved a step towards her every time she made that gesture. Finally, the horse stood right in front of Maria Rosa and let her stroke its head.

"Fortuna," she whispered.

Rosmarie was watching the scene unfold. Then she remembered to look after Viktor and make sure he was alright. It was hard for Rosmarie to leave the scene. She was so curious to know what had just happened and to hear answers to all her questions. She ran into the house to find Viktor lying on the sofa. He was covered with blankets and Erhard just came in with a bowl of soup and a cup of tea. He started feeding him with spoons of tea and soup. Rosmarie smiled. The miracle had happened. She went up to her grandfathers and put her hands on their shoulders. She smiled at them.

"I have wished for a miracle that brings my family back together and unites us all in peace. It has happened."

The two old men looked at her in surprise. She gave them a smile, skipped towards the terrace door, and went outside. There, the two women were sitting on the terrace. The horse was grazing. The sun looked out between the clouds and let the steam rise up off the meadows. It was a magical picture: a white horse standing in the steam from the meadows in the sunlight, with the green wood in the background.

Rosmarie sat down with the others.

"They saved me," she said. "I had fallen into the ravine. The torrent washed me away, and I could not get out of the flood. But they came and pulled me out."

Rosmarie saw how shocked her grandmother was to hear that. Then Maria Rosa thanked Mary Rose for saving her granddaughter.

"It was a great honour for me," Mary Rose replied. "I am here to repay a debt. I am the granddaughter of Annemarie, the woman to whom you gave your horse Fortuna in a stormy night during the war. You saved her life. The horse saved her life more than once. You both - Maria Rosa and Fortuna - saved her hope and her trust in the good in the world. She never forgot you. She thought of you every single day of her life. But life has its troubles, and she was not able to bring your horse back. Now she has sent me to return 'the unicorns' fortune,' as she calls it - the blessings of the white horse that embodies hope, trust, love and courage. Here I am, and I am honoured and grateful to thank you in the name of my grandmother and my family for everything you have done for her. She asked me to give you this letter, this book and the horse. Her name is Fortune's Bliss. She is Fortuna's great-grand daughter."

Mary Rose handed Maria Rosa a letter and a book.

Rosmarie was still puzzled. What was she talking about? Why had nobody ever told her that her grand-mother had once owned a horse? What happened in that stormy night during the war?

Grandmother Maria Rosa read the letter. She held one hand to her heart, the other hand holding the letter. She cried and cried, and in between she said: "thank you" to Mary Rose many times. After she finished reading the letter, she was finally able to stop crying. She smiled. She gently put both hands on Mary Rose's cheeks and kissed her forehead.

SAVING THE UNICORN

$\mathcal{W}$hen Rosmarie looked up, she noticed both her grandfathers standing in the doorway. Viktor sat in the lighter wheelchair her grandmother usually used when she wanted to go out. Erhard stood right behind him. They were both watching the scene. Then Rosmarie's glance fell onto Viktor. He was staring at Maria Rosa as if he had seen a ghost. His mouth was wide open and his hands were shaking.

"Grandpa, is everything alright?"

His face was pale and he started to stammer:

"You? I thought, you were dead."

Maria Rosa turned around. She looked at Viktor for a while. Then she spoke with a whispering voice.

"Yes, it is me Viktor," she said.

"And yes, I was dead. But I came back to life. It took a long time. It took a very long time, years in fact. By the time my body came back to life and my memories finally returned, it had been so long it was too late to come back to you. I wanted to tell you so many times, but I just… I did not know how to tell you. I had fallen in love with Erhard, and you had already married Frieda. So I thought it might be better not to create so much confusion. I am sorry. I should have told you. I thought about it so many times. But I was afraid. Forgive me please."

They were looking into each others eyes for a long time. It seemed like they were reading each others' minds. After a long while, Viktor nodded. Something changed in his face. Some of its hardness seemed to melt away.

Rosmarie could not wait anymore. "So I think that Viktor and Maria Rosa want to tell us a story! I cannot wait to hear this."

In that moment, she heard the noise of an engine. Engelbert, Viktoria and Frieda had come. They must have driven all the way up to the skiing area and then set over to this mountain. That was the only way to get here now. They hugged Rosmarie. They were glad to see her alive. Rosmarie looked around and she realised that for the very first time in her life her entire family was united in one place. This was a miracle. It was a historic moment. She would take her chance and bring them all together this time.

"Let's sit down together and talk. It is about time. It is going to be the first time, that this whole family has sat around the same table. And it only required me to almost die and be saved by a unicorn and a - well, a Knight of the Unicorn."

Rosmarie took the lead and went over to the big wooden table on the terrace. The horse followed. It stood right behind Rosmarie, who sat at the table. Mary

Rose came and sat down next to her. Everybody else followed. They sat in silence at the terrace table for a while and everybody was watching the white horse, that seemed to be the Alpha and the Omega in this tangled story. Rosmarie looked around the table. For the first time ever, the whole family sat together at one table. Rosmarie smiled. It made her happy. The horse brought the whole family together.

It was quiet for a while. Viktor was still staring at Maria Rosa. Viktoria and Engelbert were still staring at both of them.

"So, Maria Rosa and Mary Rose, would you like to tell us a story of a stormy night during the war?" Rosmarie ventured, to break the awkward silence.

"Yes, and Viktor and Maria Rosa might want to tell us the story of what happened before that night," Viktoria added.

Maria Rosa was exhausted by all the things that were happening. She nodded at Viktor and he started to tell their story. Rosmarie listened carefully.

"It was during the war. The war had come all the way to our valley. An evil man was the commander over the troops in the area and they were on patrol in the highland valley because the mountain path across the pass of the Tower Gate always was a smuggling route, and now it was used by people who tried to escape to Switzerland. The commander was merciless. He sent the soldiers to take off farmers what they needed. They came and took some of our best cows. Then, one day, we received a letter saying that all horses were being called up and had to be assessed whether they would be conscripted into the army. My fiancée at that time was called Marie. She was very much in love with my grandfather's horse Fortuna. She could not bear to hand that horse to the army. So she made a plan. She had the idea one evening when she was reading an old book of sagas from the valley. In that book she read a story about a witch and a unicorn. It gave her the idea to bring the horse up into the mountains and hide it there. She decided to live with it up there and make sure the commander would not find it. I was skeptical about the plan, but she insisted. At night, she sneaked out and rode off with the horse high up into the mountains. She lived with the horse for several months in the wilderness of the mountain forests, from early spring to late September. During this time, she must have helped a few people, who had tried to escape over the mountain pass and cross the border from Austria to Switzerland. The horse had been seen only once. But that was sufficient for the commander to become suspicious and alert. I tried my very best to calm the commander and told him that it was just a saga, and that people had told those stories of creatures they claimed to have seen up in the highlands ever since. I told them it was the thin air that makes people see things that aren't real. But all my effort was in vain. Eventually, one commander sent a battalion to search the mountains. It was the end of September, and it had snowed for the first time this autumn. I was very worried. But there was nothing I could do. They kept me under surveillance because I already was under suspicion. Somebody had told them that I used to have horses, but I had sold them right before the army could see them. So I was already considered a potential traitor and a potential rebel. I could not go there and warn her, because I would have led them straight to her. So I had to stay on the farm and pray. The next thing I heard was that they had found the traitor and the horse, and that they had killed them. That's what they said."

Viktor looked at Erhard.

THE HUNTSMAN AND THE WITCH

*E*rhard nodded. Then he started to speak with a hoarse voice.

"Yes, that is true. They found Marie and shot her. But the horse escaped in a snow storm. The soldiers did not want to tell the furious commander the truth, so they lied. I was there when they found her. As the hunter in this area, they asked me - well, forced me - to guide them to the correct area. They threatened to kill my parents and my brother if I didn't help them. I tried to lead them along the wrong track, but they had a German shepherd, which followed the scent and let them directly to Marie. One of the soldiers opened fire without warning. Before I even realised what had happened, she fell into the snow and left a red puddle around her. The soldiers then turned away and walked off, following the tracks of the horse through the snow, higher up into the mountains. I ran to the woman, and she looked at me with her beautiful eyes. I did not even think. I just knew

I could not let her die. I carried her to my hut and looked after her. I cut the bullet out, which had luckily missed her heart. The second bullet was stuck in an amulet with a unicorn on it. It had saved her life. She recovered only very, very slowly, but after half a year, she started to talk again. After almost a year, her spirit seemed to start coming back. But it took a long time for her to remember and recover her memories. When she woke up the first time, she did not even know her name. She often sat there and looked at the amulet. A year after the war had ended, I discovered, quite by accident who she might be. We had no money left, but I needed to get some medication for her because she was still in a lot of pain. So she gave me the medallion. She did not want to sell it, but we had nothing else to sell anymore. I took it down to the jeweller and he bought it. Some time later, I bumped into him again and he told me that Victor's wife Frieda had bought it, and that she had claimed that this was stolen from their family treasure. I said I had found it in the forest. I guess it is the reason why Viktor hated me so much. He thought I was the one who led the soldiers to Marie, and after she died, I took the medallion off her. I am sorry for the grief you endured, Viktor."

Erhard paused for a moment before he continued talking.

"That little hint from the jeweller put me on the right track. I went to the bars in the village near Viktor's farm. I quickly found out about rumours about the disappearance of Viktor's first fiancée. Nobody knew what had happened to her. Some said she was a Jew and that she had fled to Switzerland. Others suspected that Viktor might have killed her. Others said that she had been the so called witch that had been seen in the mountains - the witch with the unicorn. This way, I found out who Marie was."

It was silent for a while with everyone digesting the story. Then after a while Maria Rosa spoke with a whispering voice. She was exhausted from the events of the day. But she wanted to continue the story.

"I had taken the horse up to the forests in the mountains. There I lived and hid away. Erhard knew I was there, and even though I had never met him, I knew that he knew. He was a huntsman, he knew the terrain and he could read the tracks. He seemed to protect me, and constantly led the soldiers the wrong way. But then, one day he came and told me that they were hunting some people who tried to escape across the mountain pass to Switzerland and they were tracking them across the woods. He said there were a lot of them. And that they used a dog to search the area. He begged me to leave the horse behind and rescue myself. He had to leave again, he said, because if he was not going to lead them, they would kill his family. He said: 'Save yourself. There will be no escape soon.' That night, all of a sudden, a snow storm swept across the mountains. It was late September, and it is not uncommon for it to snow up there in the mountains for the first time in September. That snowstorm was deadly for some - lucky for others. Many people died that night. I hid with the horse in the dense forests. But I knew they were coming closer. I could hear them. I was scared to death. I was weighing up my options. Should I go to Switzerland? Should I leave home? I was in a panic. The snowstorm howled, I was cold, I was scared, I did not know what to do. Suddenly, a woman stood in front of me. I had not heard her coming, because the storm was howling. The snow was falling in thick flakes. She was white in the face, exhausted and she could barely stand anymore. She looked at me and I could see the horror in her eyes. She was scared. She knew it was her end, there was no escape for her, they would kill her if they found her. I suddenly knew what to do: I put her on the horse's back and told the horse to go to the marketplace just over the border in Switzerland. It knew the way across the mountains. It obeyed and walked off. It was a very intelligent horse, very sensitive, too. It knew that this was a matter of life and death. The horse and the woman set off through the snowstorm. I followed their tracks to the ravine, and then I walked down through the torrent. This way, I hoped that the dog would lose my scent. It worked. The soldiers and the dog followed the tracks of the horse. But the horse was faster. It escaped. I knew it had escaped. I could feel it in my heart. Its pursuers all died in the snowstorm, their frozen bodies were found the following day. Further down the ravine, I left the water and ran into the forest where I was planning to hide. But unfortunately, there was another group of soldiers with their hounds on the track. They hunted me across the forest. I knew the mountain forests better than anyone else and for a while I thought I could escape. But the snow was deep, it was exhausting to run and I left tracks. The soldiers came ever closer. I could hear the hounds howling. I thought the only way to escape the hounds would be to cross the ravine and climb up the steep rock walls on the other side. There the hounds could not follow me. So I took the route down to the ravine. I climbed down, crossed the icy torrent and started to climb up on the other side. I was close to the top when a soldier shot me. A bullet hit me and I fell into the ravine. I lay in the snow and saw the soldiers above. One soldier looked at me and then he shot another bullet that hit me at my chest. The soldiers turned around, they just left me there to die. But Erhard came. He kneeled down beside me. That was the last thing I remembered. When I woke up, I did not know where I was, what happened, or who I was. Nothing. I could neither walk, nor could I talk. It took a long time to recover. I learned to talk again and to move my body. But I could never really walk again. I could hardly stand up. After some time, memories started to come back. In the beginning, it was just a dream ever so often. Then the dreams came more often, sometimes during the days. But it took a long time to solve the puzzle. We had to keep it a secret that I was alive, and we could not tell anyone about it. Erhard said there were so many collaborators amongst our own folks, that we could not trust anybody. So we kept the secret. We just lived up here together, the two of us. We lived a simple and secluded life. Erhard hid me from the commander and he cared for me. After the war, we made up a story, that I was his fiancée from Switzerland, where he had met me at the marketplace on the other side of the mountains. We made up a new identity for me. I chose the name Maria Rosa. I coloured my hair, cut it and kept it short and straight. In all these years, I have never been down to the valley. I think I was so traumatised by what had happened that I never wanted to go there again. But also,

I was in a wheelchair and I was in a lot of pain. Up here in the mountain forest I felt safe. It became my home. I wanted to stay here." Maria Rosa sighed. She looked tired.

"I think that is enough for today. You should get some sleep. We can pick this up tomorrow at breakfast if you like?" Erhard looked worried at his exhausted wife.

"Yes, you should rest grandma. Go to bed." Rosmarie did not feel like ending this get-together, but she saw that her grandmother was worn out.

Mary Rose was invited to stay with them in the cabin tonight and so was Engelbert. Viktoria, Frieda and Viktor returned to their cabin on the other side of the highland valley. They wished each other goodnight, and for the first time in her life, Rosmarie said goodnight to her whole family at once. Then they drove off and she took her grandmother to bed and gave her a hug and a kiss.

"Grandma Maria Rosa, you are a very brave woman. I am proud to have such a grandmother."

Maria Rosa smiled. Then she closed her eyes and fell asleep.

THE DARKEST NIGHT AND THE
MAGIC HORSE

he following morning, Rosmarie woke up early. It was still a bit windy and rainy. She went downstairs and found Maria Rosa was still sleeping. She went outside. Erhard had already given the horse water and hay. The horse seemed to be happy and ate its hay next to the donkey, the cow, the sheep, the goats and the orphaned baby deer that Erhard raised with a bottle. It seemed to be in good company and enjoyed the tasty hay made from mountain meadows. Since the horse had its breakfast already, Rosmarie went to the back of the shed where the chicken and the geese were. She collected the eggs and returned to the house. The clouds opened and the sun shone, so she laid the table outside on the veranda. She made a big breakfast with everything they had, and sent her mother and her grandparents a message to say that breakfast was ready and that she was expecting them.

Engelbert was the next one to rise. Mary Rose and

Maria Rosa were both still sleeping. They must have been exhausted and overwhelmed by all that had happened. A little later Viktor, Frieda and Viktoria arrived. Mary Rose and Maria Rosa were awoken by the sound of the car and they came to the breakfast table.

Rosmarie was happy. This was what she had wished for: to bring the family back together. And more than that, her other lifelong wish had come true: they had a family horse now! And she had a new friend. A friend like none she had ever had before. If there was such a thing as a soulmate, then for sure, Mary Rose was hers. They must have had related souls. Rosmarie had never met anyone before to whom she felt so close without knowing her. They shared their love for horses. It was as if they were some sort of twin sisters in spirit: Mary Rose and Rosmarie.

After breakfast, Rosmarie took the book that Maria Rosa had received from Mary Rose. She curled up on the sofa and started reading out loud. Everybody was listening. Maria Rosa and Erhard sat there hand in hand, in a way that Rosmarie had not seen them do ever before. The appearance of the horse and the Scottish woman seemed to bond them even stronger. And Mary Rose seemed to be connected to her grandmother in a way that Rosmarie almost envied. It upset her a little bit that she seemed to know everything whilst Rosmarie had been completely oblivious all those years. But she tried to let go of those feelings. She knew that the war had left deep wounds and left its scars on her grandparents, but it had also created an invisible bond between those that had held together in these times.

None of her grandparents ever talked about that

time. It had shaken the foundations of society, humanity, and her family. During the war, the unthinkable had become reality. The world had been turned upside down. Evil took over and destroyed everything that did not suit its purpose. All her grandparents had been young people at this time, and maybe it had destroyed all their hopes and dreams and faith in the good of the world. Rosmarie could understand why they wanted to forget. That was why they never talked about it. That was why, they had not told her.

She turned the page and started reading.

A miracle has happened. I made it across the mountains to Switzerland. And I am alive! I cannot believe it. All that happened is so surreal, I couldn't believe it myself. I would tell myself, I was hallucinating from hunger, the cold and the exhaustion, if that horse hadn't been standing right here, next to me.I keep touching it and stroking it, as it is the only thing I have and I need to reassure myself every few minutes that it is real, that it is alive and that I am alive too. I cannot believe it. I am so surprised and relieved, that for the first time in months, my fear is gone. Fear was with me all the time. It had become my normal and permanent state. But now, I have that horse. And every time I am scared, I look at it and touch it. And the fear goes away. It is magic.

Fortuna is the name of the horse, the woman said. Fortuna, what an appropriate name. Without that horse, I wouldn't have made it. Without that horse, I would have given up. Without that horse, I would have died. That horse has a strength I admire. Every time I feel like I want to just lay down and die, the horse gives me that look. It knows what I am thinking. It can read my mind. It feels it. And it somehow, magically, awakens within me what I need most: hope, strength and an unbreakable will to live. I don't know, how it does it. It is magic. This horse is magic. Maybe it really is a unicorn.

That thought helped me through the snowstorm. It was so cold, and I was so exhausted and so close to death. My body was almost frozen, I couldn't see anything and I knew I was almost dead. My only hope to survive was that horse. I knew, I needed to trust it and hold on to its mane and stay on its back. I lost hope and death was creeping into my bones with the cold. So my mind decided to escape into a fairy tale. I was a princess and I was riding a unicorn. The ice queen was trying to kill us, but I knew the magical unicorn would save me and bring me into the magical land called Switzerland. We both wanted to escape from the evil soldiers that were hunting us.

"I trust you! Unicorn, save us," I said to the unicorn - only in thoughts, because my face was frozen and I could not speak out loud. But I knew already, that the unicorn could read my mind. The unicorn fought its way through the snowstorm. It was impossible to see anything. But still it pressed on, one step after the other. Unerringly, it kept going. I was lying on its back and trying to hold onto its mane with my frozen fingers. I lost any sense of time, space and I even lost sensation in my body. I couldn't feel my fingers, nor my face, nor my feet. I knew I was so close to death. I started sliding, slowly, because I couldn't go on anymore and I thought I just wanted to die.

In that moment the horse turned its head around and looked at me. It was saying:

"Get yourself together and hang on. We are not giving up just like that."

I got myself together and tried to stay alive for another second. And one more second. And one more.

When I woke up, I was lying in a warm soft bed. At first, I thought I was dead. But when I opened my eyes a woman sat down besides my bed and told me that I was alive, which was a miracle. She said, I was in Switzerland. I started to cry, I was so relieved. She said a white horse had carried me through the snowstorm and stopped right in front of their house. The horse saved me. This horse is a miracle.

Rosmarie put the book down. She was amazed. She looked at the circle of people at the table: everybody seemed to be astonished. They all had listened in awe.

"Fortuna saved this woman!" Viktor said out loud. "She found the path over the Tower Gate to Switzerland in the snow storm. And she brought her to - I bet it was Mrs. Berger. She loved Fortuna and always gave her an apple. Fortuna really was an amazing horse."

There was silence for a moment. Then Viktor continued. He was looking at Maria Rosa and he said:

"You have done the right thing. You have shown courage."

Grandmother Maria Rosa nodded gratefully to Viktor. It meant that he had forgiven her.

Then Viktor turned to Mary Rose. "And your grandmother went all the way to Scotland? By horse?"

"Yes, in her diary, you can read about her journey. She was exhausted and Fortuna took the lead at some point. She walked all across Great Britain, straight to Scotland, directly onto my grandfather's land. She stayed for her entire life. She was deeply traumatised, and it took a long time until she felt better. My grandfather said that for years she would wake up at night in fear. I think it was always on her mind to return Fortuna. But the years went by, and at some point the horse died. She grew very old and lived a long and happy life. She had three foals. One day, she fell asleep on the pasture and never got up again. My mother was born and life took its course. So time went by. But she never forgot about you, Maria Rosa. She told me stories, when I was a child. She told me about her homeland of Austria, and how beautiful it was with its mountains, lakes, rivers and forests. She told me the story of her flight at least a hundred times. The highlight of the story is the moment when she thinks she is going to die, and she meets a woman in the forest, who gives her her horse that takes her across the border to Switzerland in the snowstorm. You were very brave and generous, and my grandmother owes you her life. More than this, my grandmother was in a state of deep anxiety. She had thought she could not trust anyone. Then she met you. For her, that was a bright light in a dark night. She says the horse embodies this bright light - the light of love. It shines at night in the moonlight. And it gives her hope and takes away her fear. When she realised this she knew that she wanted to repay her dept. She must have had it on her mind for years. On the morning of my eighteenth birthday, she asked me to fulfill her last wish: to return the fortune of the unicorn to the woman who gave it to her."

FORTUNE'S BLISS

The next day, Mary Rose woke up early. The sun shone on her bed. She got up and went outside. It was a beautiful morning. She stepped onto the terrace of the cabin. Maria Rosa sat in her wheelchair in the middle of the meadow and the horse danced around her. Rosmarie was standing next to them, giving them gentle instructions. She had taught her grandmother Liberty Training from the wheelchair! Mary Rose was very touched. It was so amazing to see the magic unfold. Rosmarie was enchanted straight away by Fortune's Bliss, and she was eager to learn everything about horsemanship and horse training. She quickly learned the lessons Mary Rose taught her, and now, she was already teaching her grandmother. It was fascinating to see how the horse spread a glittering trail of magic wherever it went. Fortune's Bliss had always been a horse that knew its duties and maybe it had now found its purpose. It looked like that after all. She created magic wherever she went and quickly managed to enchant the whole family.

Mary Rose turned around when she heard steps behind her. Erhard stepped onto the terrace and watched his wife and granddaughter dancing with the horse. He put his hand on Mary Roses's shoulder.

"Thank you," he said.

Mary Rose gave him a smile.

"It is a real pleasure to watch them. I have to thank you." She put her hand on the hand of Erhard on her shoulder, and they watched together the horse dancing with the two women.

Mary Rose took some pictures. Then she went inside with a smile. Erhard had offered her the use of his computer. So she sat down and she started writing an email to her grandmother, which she sent to George, who would print it out and give it to her. She added the pictures and then sent it. Finally, she took the phone and called her grandmother.

"Grandma! Guess where I am! I am here! I found them. You were so right about everything. I came at just the right moment. They love the horse. It's brought the whole family back together. I wish you could be here! It is so amazing to watch them and their pure joy with the horse. You should come over here. You should see it for yourself! It is lovely!"

Mary Rose spoke to Annemarie on the phone and told her about all the wonderful things that had happened, and the magic that was unfolding through the presence of the horse. Annemarie was very happy to hear that. She was relieved and was moved to tears. She thanked Mary Rose many times. After the long phone call she sounded weak and tired, so Mary Rose offered to call her again soon and told her she should get some rest.

Annemarie said: "Thank you, darling Mary Rose. I love you." Then she hung up.

Mary Rose went outside, and watched Rosmarie and Maria Rosa who were still enthralled by dancing with the horse. After a while the dance ended and the horse started to graze. Both women watched the horse. It seemed that they could not take their eyes off the horse. Rosmarie especially could not get enough. She sat close to it and watched it grazing. After a while she stroked it. Then she sat on its back and rode without a saddle or reins. She could navigate the horse with just her weight and a gentle touch of her legs. Mary Rose had taught her how to stop the horse by just slightly blocking her hip and no longer swinging with the horse's movement. The horse slowed immediately, and when she slightly pressed her knees together it stopped even from a trot.

Rosmarie's cheeks were red, and a smile spread across her face. She had always loved horses, and she had always longed for one. And then, all of a sudden, her grandmother received the most beautiful horse she could ever have wished for. Not only was it beautiful, it had a great character, gentle and yet spirited. On top of that, it was exceptionally well trained. Rosmarie had never seen a horse that reacted to such tiny gestures. She remembered how Mary Rose just pointed with one finger and inclined her head to make the horse kneel down. She wanted to learn all of this.

Mary Rose was relieved when she watched Rosmarie in such blissful happiness. It was clear that she had longed for that horse so long and she seemed eternally happy in this moment. Mary Rose was very glad to see that. She herself loved Fortune's Bliss very much, and was glad to see that she was in good hands here. She smiled at Rosmarie's enthusiasm. As soon as she had learned an exercise, she was eager to master the next. Fortune's Bliss seemed happy with Rosmarie - of course, that was pure love the horse was receiving. The horse knew that this woman already had given it her heart. She would do anything for that horse. The horse sensed that, and was in turn willing to do anything for her. Without hesitation she followed Rosmarie's gentle prompts. Rosmarie seemed to be a skilled and fearless rider. Mary Rose had seen enough. She knew that here was a woman who was born to ride the unicorn.

The horse dropped into a canter according to Rosmarie's guidance. The white horse was galloping across the meadow in full bloom. The sun shone through the clouds and the silhouette of the horse and the woman, flying over the land, looked amazing. Maria Rosa and Erhard watched her with a smile. So did Mary Rose. The horse flew across the meadow and the woman flew with it on its back. It looked very much like a fairy tale. They were flying, leaving a glittering trail of magic in their wake.

That night, Mary Rose could not sleep. She was too excited and too happy to have completed the mission. Her main concern that the people who would receive her horse were not competent handlers, had now been well and truly assuaged. She felt very relieved. At the same time however, she was worried. Her grandmother had been tired and had not spoken much. She had called uncle Gordon thereafter. He had said that she was weak and that the doctor had visited. She thought about her grandmother. She got up and looked out of the window. A beautiful full moon shone through the starlit sky. The moon was big, round and white, shining on the peaks of the mountains. The moonlight reflected off the fur of the horse and it made it shine in the night. It was an amazing view. She prayed for her grandmother. Then she went to bed again. When she finally fell asleep late at night, she had a dream. She dreamed she saw her grandmother flying on the back of a white horse across the sky.

SAVIOURS OF LOVE

*M*ary Rose sat at the grave of her grandparents and looked to the horizon. The sea was quiet and peaceful. A gentle breeze blew from the ocean up the cliff and through her hair. She opened the letter that grandmother Annemarie had left for her. She found it on her bed when she came back to their cottage in Scotland. She started reading.

Dear Mary Rose,

When you receive this letter, I will already be gone. I am sorry that I could not hold on for your return. But I have had so much time in this world, my time has come to go. Tonight there is a full moon. The sky is blue and black, and the moon shines bright. It is the light of the moon, that lights the darkest night. The light of the moon makes the sea shine. The light of the moon makes the horses glow in the night. And it makes my heart glow as well, when I look at this magical landscape.

As I am looking into the moonlight now, I know that you

are somewhere in the Alps, looking at the light of the moon, shining over the white peaks of the mountains, and making the horse glow in the dark. I know that this light shines in your heart as well. You have proven it. That is the true purpose of the mission, I wanted to light the light in your heart, and make you truly understand how important this is. I really hope that you will pass on the light of love to somebody else - maybe your partner, your children or grandchildren, and of course, you have already brought it back to my saviour and her family. I am very proud of you. Keep the light of love, and light it in as many hearts as you possibly can.

As I know you and Fortune's Bliss, I am convinced that you already have lit up hearts all along your trail. Everybody who has seen you is enchanted. It's the purpose of the mission: spreading the light of love all along the way. Love is the most valuable thing we have, and the most important thing in the world. We sometimes forget that. Sometimes the fear is so big, that we cannot feel love anymore. Sometimes even the days are filled with worries, pain and suffering. In those moments, we need love and light more than ever. Love is magic. It possesses power. With a light of love you can enchant your world.

You have become a knight. You are a rider of those magic horses that seem to embody light, love and hope. You repaid my dept and returned the gift to my saviour. You are brave, wise and kind. You are a knight of the light of love.

Last night I dreamed that I stood at the window and watched the moonlight and the sea. I saw a white horse that cantered across the sky above the sea in the moonlight. It landed at the top of the cliff. It looked at me. I knew it was

Fortuna, my magic horse. She had come to pick me up and take me across the sky.

I am looking forward to the ride across the sky on the back of my beloved horse, that always kept me safe and led me through the darkest times. My time has come. I must say goodbye to you now. I know you will find your way, you are a strong woman. I love you. I will always be in your heart. Just remember, whatever happens, save the light of love.

Yours, Annemarie

Mary Rose cried, but her grandmother's words made her smile at the same time. She had a view from the cliff over the sea to the horizon. The sky opened above her. The moon was there - a white ball in the blue sky. It made Mary Rose smile.

The horses were grazing nearby. When they lifted their heads, Mary Rose knew that somebody was coming. Mary Rose did not turn around. She just sat there and looked to the horizon. Somebody sat down next to her and touched her shoulder.

"Hei, Darling."

It was her mother. Somebody sat down to her other side. It was her father. They hugged her from both sides, and held her in their arms. Mary Rose was glad they had come. They cried together, and then they sat and told each other stories of grandmother Annemarie. Mary Rose had not felt that close to her parents in a long time.

ABOUT THE AUTHOR

BARBARA SCHÖNHER

Barbara Schönher was born on a snowy December day in the early 1980s in a small town in the Austrian Alps. She was born under the sign of Sagittarius - the archer, half horse, half human - in a town called Bludenz that has the unicorn as emblem on its flag. She is a descendent of mountain farmers that always kept horses, who were horsemen for many generations, whose family emblem is the unicorn. Somehow she was magically drawn to horses. As soon as she could talk and walk, she convinced her mother that she just needed to ride. As soon as she could ride and write, she started writing horse stories. And that is what she loved doing the most: writing and riding.

One day her grandmother told her mother she should buy a horse, because she could see how much her granddaughters were longing for one. Her mother bought a horse for the family. They spent many happy years together and the horse saved her more than once.

It was a magic horse that carried her safely from childhood to adulthood, through the storms of life, across mountains and rivers, and it never let her down. In the year 2000 when she herself turned 18, she started to write a story about a young woman that was enchanted by the unicorn and empowered by her love for horses. But somehow she did not finish it, she went to study, and after her magic horse sadly passed away, she stopped writing and she quit riding. She just couldn't anymore. She left Austria and lived abroad for a couple of years. One day, when she travelled through Scotland, she noticed the unicorn emblem on the flag. It was calling her. The unicorn appeared to her again and again, wherever she went. She had left her hometown and the place of her family where the unicorn was omnipresent and everything reminded her of the loss of her magic horse, but wherever she went, it was there: the unicorn. It was her calling. She knew it. Every time she saw a unicorn, she felt something moving deep inside her. It was the knowing that she carried an unfinished story within. So she dug out her old story and continued to write it. It was her story, the story of the woman who could sense the magic of horses and who saw a unicorn in every horse. She knew she owed it to the horses to tell the world the truth about unicorns. In her words:

"The truth is, there is a unicorn in every horse, and every horse can bring magic to your life. It is up to you to become a knight of the unicorn and a human that is worthy of the fellowship of the unicorn. If your are honest and kind, if your horse decides you can be trusted, one day when you least expect it, it will take you to its magic world and show you the

beauty of life. So keep your heart honest and kind and a unicorn might appear in your life."

She knew she was lucky having had a magic horse that took her to its magical land and never let her down. If she could do one thing in return for the horses, she would try to convince people to treat them with more respect. Her way of doing that was to write this story.

Writing this story was a healing process for her. Shortly after she started to write again, she also started to ride again. The moment she sat on a horseback for the first time, years after her horse had died, she felt whole again. It was like coming home. She knew that from now on she would always ride and she knew she needed to have a horse again. So she decided to finish writing this story, to publish it as her first book.

This is the first one of her stories she came out with, her debut novel. Sometimes she is tempted to believe that it is her calling to write human-horse-stories. After all, wasn't that what the unicorn tried to tell her?

AUTHOR WEBSITE

Thank you for buying this book!

If you liked this story, please support me in my quest of becoming an author. I am an independent author and solely rely on my readers' support and the word of mouth for the promotion of my book. Please leave a review and tell your friends about this book.

If you want to stay in touch and receive the latest news please sign up to my newsletter via the contact page of my website barbaraschoenher.com and you will be the first to know when the next story comes out and you will receive information about special offers.

Please give me a like on Facebook by following the link on my website.

ACKNOWLEDGMENTS

Special thanks to my language editors:
Dr. Nick Dommett & Dr. Ralph Beeby
& Sheila McDaniel.

A big thanks for editing the content to Martina.

Thanks to my test-readers: Birgit, Pia & Nicole.

Special thanks to Katharina Schönher for designing the
cover picture.